The thing about Kate, he'd discovered, was that she refused to be beaten by what life threw at her. She kept going, kept smiling, always positive, always upbeat, seeing the best in situations, the best in people.

Angus was not sure where all this rational thinking was getting him, although he now had a much fuller picture of the woman he loved.

Loved?

He set the cup back carefully in its saucer, certain it had been about to slip from his grasp.

Loved?

How could he love her? He barely knew her. But even as this excuse sprang from his brain, another part of his mind was denying it. Of course he knew her.

He pictured her on the yellow sofa, an arm around his son, and remembered the stab of jealousy he'd felt. But what he should have felt was pleasure—that finally he'd found a woman who would make the ideal mother for his son…

CHRISTMAS AT JIMMIE'S

At Jimmie's Children's Unit,
miracles don't just happen at Christmas
time—babies are saved every day!

But this year there are two children
with some big wishes for Santa…

BACHELOR OF THE BABY WARD
—little Hamish McDowell
wants a new mummy…

FAIRYTALE ON THE CHILDREN'S WARD
—all Emily Jackson longs for
is to see her mum and dad reunited…

*Will Hamish and Emily
get the greatest Christmas gifts of all?*

Find out in Meredith Webber's heartwarming
linked duet, out this month!

BACHELOR OF
THE BABY WARD

BY
MEREDITH WEBBER

First published in Great Britain 2010
Large Print edition 2011
Harlequin Mills & Boon Limited,
Eton House, 18-24 Paradise Road,
Richmond, Surrey TW9 1SR

© Meredith Webber 2010

ISBN: 978 0 263 21728 5

Harlequin Mills & Boon policy is to use papers that are
natural, renewable and recyclable products and made
from wood grown in sustainable forests. The logging and
manufacturing process conform to the legal environmental
regulations of the country of origin.

Printed and bound in Great Britain
by CPI Antony Rowe, Chippenham, Wiltshire

Meredith Webber says of herself, 'Some ten years ago, I read an article which suggested that Mills and Boon were looking for new Medical™ Romance authors. I had one of those "I can do that" moments, and gave it a try. What began as a challenge has become an obsession—though I do temper the "butt on seat" career of writing with dirty but healthy outdoor pursuits, fossicking through the Australian Outback in search of gold or opals. Having had some success in all of these endeavours, I now consider I've found the perfect lifestyle.'

Recent titles by the same author:

DESERT KING, DOCTOR DADDY
GREEK DOCTOR: ONE MAGICAL CHRISTMAS
CHILDREN'S DOCTOR, MEANT-TO-BE WIFE*
THE HEART SURGEON'S SECRET CHILD†

*Crocodile Creek
†Jimmie's Children's Unit

CHAPTER ONE

'But I'd assumed—'

A quick frown from her boss, Alex Attwood, failed to halt Kate Armstrong's angry protest.

'—that when Phil and Maggie left to go back to England, I'd take Maggie's place as anaesthetist on *your* team, not be working with some total stranger.'

Alex's frown turned to a sigh.

'Have you any idea how hard it is to juggle so many new people on the two teams?' he asked, only slight exasperation showing in his voice. 'I've left you in the second team—and you know darned well that doesn't mean second in importance—because you know the ropes and you'll be a help to Angus, whom, by the way, you should meet!'

Alex paused to grin at her.

'That way he won't be a *total* stranger!' He turned towards the door behind Kate and added, 'Come on in, Angus. We were just discussing you.'

Kate was torn between wishing the floor would open up and swallow her, and wondering why a quick, embarrassed glance at a tall, dark-haired stranger should make her stomach feel uneasy.

Angus McDowell had more on his mind than some redheaded termagant—one of his mother's favourite words—who obviously didn't want to work with him. Hamish had thrown out a rash, the quarantine kennels had phoned to say McTavish was sick and, as he'd left the house, Juanita had given him a shopping list a mile long, telling him that as she didn't know where the supermarket was—he'd have to find one.

But apparently the termagant was going to be working with him whether she liked it or not, so he offered her a practiced smile, and held out his hand, politely ignored the fiery blush that had swept into her cheeks.

'Angus McDowell,' he said as she slipped fine-boned fingers into his clasp, then quickly withdrew them, tucking her hand into the pocket of her jacket as if to save it further contamination.

'Kate Armstrong,' she said, her voice deeper than he would have expected in a small, slim woman. Slightly husky, too, the voice, although maybe that was a hangover from the argument she'd been having with Alex. 'I'm to be your anaesthetist.'

It had to be jet lag that made Angus feel a splinter of ice run through his veins—she wasn't talking about anaesthetising *him*! He pulled himself together and managed another smile.

'Great,' he said. 'Most important part of the team, the anaesthetist—well, alongside the perfusionist—'

'And the second surgeon, and the surgical assistant, and the scrub nurse, and the circulating—'

He held up his hands in surrender.

'You're right, we're a team, and every member of it is equally important, although your job carries a lot of pressure, because you have more pre-

and post-op contact with the patient and his or her parents.'

She looked at him then—really looked—pale green eyes meeting his, offering a challenge.

'Soft-soaping me?' she said, softening the challenge with a slight smile. 'You obviously heard the argument I was having with Alex.'

She shrugged, shoulders in a crisp white shirt lifting slightly.

'It was nothing personal—not against you. I'd just been looking forward to working with Alex. Not that I haven't done ops with him—we all switch around from time to time—but I find I learn different things from different surgeons.'

It sounded weak and Angus wondered if there was some other reason this woman wanted to be on Alex's team—a personal reason. But he couldn't be worrying about such things when he had enough personal problems of his own to sort out.

Hamish for one, even apart from the rash…

He shut off the dark cloud of the past, concentrating on the present. He said, 'Then I hope you will find working with me as instructive.'

He moved away from her as other members of the team filtered into the room.

Kate looked around at the newcomers. She'd met Oliver Rankin, the new paediatric surgical fellow who would be working with both teams, a few months ago when he'd spent several weeks with the paediatric cardiac surgical unit at Jimmie's—as the St James Hospital for Children was affectionately known. But this was the first time she'd seen Clare Jackson, the new perfusionist, and from the way every male eye in the room turned to Clare as she walked in, the perfusionist was going to cause a stir in the tight-knit unit.

Admittedly it wasn't Clare's fault that she was tall, dark-haired and strikingly beautiful. Kate tugged at her scraggly red locks which, no matter how she tried to tame them, were always breaking out of their confinement, and wondered what it would be like to be beautiful, to be so much the centre of attention....

Not that she'd like the attention part.

The talk had turned to patients, those who had been operated on and their progress, before moving to a rough plan for the operations for the week. Rough because no-one ever knew when some baby would be born with a congenital heart defect that would need immediate attention.

'Angus, we've been advised of a baby with a TGA coming down from a regional hospital on the north coast hopefully tomorrow,' Alex said. 'They want to stabilise him before the airlift. I know you've made something of a speciality of transposition of the great arteries so I'd like your team to take him when he comes.'

The new surgeon nodded, though Kate noticed he looked worried at the same time. Surely he couldn't be concerned about the operation, not if he specialised in it and when it was one that was performed successfully so often these days.

The little frown between his eyes made him more human somehow, Kate decided, studying the face that had at first appeared stern and unyielding to her. Was it the darkness of his hair and eyes that made him seem that way, or the strong bones beneath olive skin that stretched tightly over them so the long nose between broad cheekbones and the firm jawbone were accentuated?

'Kate, you with us?'

She looked across at Alex and nodded, though she'd have liked to bite him for drawing attention to her momentary lapse in concentration.

'Of course!' she snapped.

'Then off you go. Take Angus down to the child-care centre, and when you've finished there, give him a general tour of the area. Apparently he's got some shopping to do.'

She looked from Alex to the stranger with whom she was going to be working, really regretting now that she'd missed the bit of the conversation where she'd been stuck with being his tour guide. Angus was on his feet and coming towards her, smiling again....

The smile, though it seemed practiced and didn't quite reach his eyes, caused another weird sensation in the pit of her stomach. Although maybe that was the slightly mouldy bread she'd used for toast that morning. But just in case, she turned away from the smile and hurried out of the room, assuming he would follow.

'You've children yourself that Alex appointed you to show me the childcare centre?'

If she'd been a sucker for accents this one would have won her over, a soft Scottish burr overlaid with a little bit of North American. The effect in the deep voice was totally enthralling.

'Children?' he repeated, and she knew she had to pull herself together.

'Not yet,' she said, 'but I'd like to have a family and I'd also like to keep working, at least part-time, so somehow I became involved—'

She was used enough to this conversational subject to be able to keep her voice casually light, but they'd reached the elevator foyer and she could no longer pretend she had to look where she was going, so had to turn to face him.

'—with a move to expand the hours of the centre. It made sense to me to have it open twenty-four hours a day, so people on night shifts, or staff called in unexpectedly at night as our team often is, have somewhere to leave their children.'

Definitely too much information but the uneasiness in her stomach—not to mention the disturbing shadows she now saw in his dark eyes—had her prattling on.

The elevator arrived and they crammed inside, the conversation, fortunately, ceasing as they rode down to the ground floor where most of the passengers exited.

'It's in the basement?' Angus queried, wondering about the reasoning behind keeping children in a dingy, dark environment.

His reluctant guide—he'd seen her sigh when Alex suggested she take him around—smiled, small, even white teeth gleaming in her pale face.

'Ah, but there are basements and basements?'

'Mostly, in hospitals, used for the morgue,' he reminded her, while he wondered why small, even teeth should have made such an impression on him.

Teeth?

Surely he wasn't developing a tooth fetish.

'Not here,' she said cheerfully, leading him out

of the elevator and along a wide corridor decorated with a bright mural depicting zoo animals.

She pushed open a door and they entered a small, fenced-off foyer, beyond which Angus could see a big, bright room, bright because the whole of one wall was glass, and beyond the glass was a playground—a sunlit playground!

'We're in a basement?' he queried as he took in the children in groups around tables in the big room, and beyond it another room with a wide window so he could see cots set up within it.

'The hospital is built on a hill. It wasn't hard to excavate a little more on this side so the children had an outdoor area.'

A woman came towards them, greeting Kate with genuine delight.

'You've been a stranger,' she said. 'After you did so much to help get the after-hours arrangement set up, we all felt you were part of our team.'

To Angus's surprise, Kate Armstrong looked embarrassed by the praise, but she rallied and introduced him.

'Mary is the director of the centre,' Kate

explained, 'so if you want to get your children in, she's the one you need to talk to.'

'Of course, the children of hospital staff get priority but we do take in children from the local area, as well,' Mary explained. 'You'll be looking for something—for how many children and what ages?'

'Just the one,' Angus replied. 'Hamish is four and moving to Australia is a big change in his life. I feel if he can make some friends here, he'll settle in more easily.'

'Of course he will,' Mary assured him. 'And we can take another child in our four-year-old group. In fact, we'll be particularly happy to have a boy, as we're a bit top-heavy with girls in that group. Would you like to come in and look around now, or would some other time suit you? Perhaps a time when you can bring your wife?'

Angus closed his eyes briefly. There always came a moment! He shored up the defences he'd built around his heart and answered calmly.

'I'm a single parent,' he said, happy the phrase was so familiar these days that no questions followed it. 'But as Kate's been seconded to show me where the supermarket is, and I don't want to take up too much of her time,' he added to Mary, 'perhaps I could come back this afternoon?'

'Any time,' she said. 'And you're in good hands with Kate. If anyone knows her way around a supermarket, it's our Dr Armstrong.'

'Why would she say that?' he asked his guide as they walked back to the elevator.

The redhead shrugged, looking thoroughly embarrassed once again. He knew it must be her colouring but it was unusual—refreshing?—to see a woman blush these days. But as they waited for the elevator, she shook off her embarrassment and explained.

'When the childcare centre first asked the hospital powers that be about extending hours, the usual objections were raised—costs, and where would the money come from, et cetera—so a few of us, mostly parents and childcare centre staff, began to fund-raise with the aim of getting enough money to trial the idea. We baked a lot of cakes over a couple of months, selling them within the hospital to patients, visitors and staff. We used the kindergarten kitchen after hours and as my hours were fairly erratic—and to be perfectly honest I'm not much of a biscuit or cake cook—I was the chief shopper.'

'And you don't have children?'

The elevator had arrived but she didn't move, looking at him again, the defiance in her eyes echoed in the slight tilt of her chin.

'No, but that's not to say I won't ever have them.'

Did she feel she'd been too adamant that she added quickly, 'And a lot of the people involved in the fund-raising were my friends.'

They rode back up to the ground floor, the questions he'd have liked to ask—was she married, did her husband work at the hospital—were too personal when they'd just met. There was something about her—pale skin, delicate features and a slim dancer's body, straight-backed, head held high—that reminded him of the delicate porcelain figurines his mother collected, so he kept sneaking looks at her.

At least, he thought that's why he kept looking at her. It had to be; he didn't look at women any other way these days—well, not often, and definitely not at women who were colleagues.

Yet he was intrigued enough to ask the questions anyway.

'You seem positive about the children in your future. Are you already married to their father? Engaged?'

They were walking through a fairly crowded foyer so someone bumped into her when she stopped abruptly and he had to put out his hand to grab her shoulder and steady her. But the people around them didn't seem to bother her as she studied him for a moment, then gave a rueful smile, cheeks pink again.

'Not married, not even engaged, but all I've wanted to be since I was eleven is a grandmother, and, being a doctor, I do understand I'll have to be a mother first.'

She'd made a joke of it, but underneath her light-hearted confession, Angus sensed a deeper emotion and wondered if this was a stock answer she gave to fend off further questions. It must have some basis in truth, so what had happened when she was eleven?

And why was he wondering?

Then she added, 'Maybe,' and the word had such sad undertones he wanted to hug her—a comforting hug, nothing more, but not something he made a habit of doing with colleagues.

It was strange that the man's questions had Kate coming out with something she'd never told a soul, not even her best friend. And while it was true it *had* been an ambition since childhood, she'd blurted it out it because the pang she always felt when the question of children arose had surprised her today with its intensity.

Had he fallen for the grandmother excuse? Who would? A diversion—that's what she needed.

'There's a coffee shop here that does good coffee and great friands, a sort of pastry. Let's fortify ourselves for the shopping trip.'

She waved her hand in the direction of the coffee shop, then realised half the hospital could be taking a break there. Walking in with a man who'd immediately be established in the hospital's top-ten most handsome could give rise to the kind of gossip she hated.

'No, a better idea would be to show you the best little eating place around here. The breakfast crowd will have gone and the morning coffee crowd not arrived. It's a bit of a walk but through a nice park. Come on.'

What was she doing? It had to be more than strangeness in her stomach from mouldy bread that had her confessing her grandmother obsession to the man one minute, then asking him to Scoozi for coffee the next.

Someone in the hospital coffee shop she didn't want to see? Angus wondered, but he followed her out of the hospital, across a road and into the big park that stretched away for what seemed like miles.

'I've a hospital house down that road,' he said, pointing across the intersection where solid, old, two- and three-storeyed houses lined a tree-shaded street. 'My house is opposite a park. Is this the same park?'

His guide turned towards him, a frown on her face—a face which, unlike his mother's porcelain figurines, showed every emotion.

Right now it was a picture of dismayed disbelief.

'You're living in one of the hospital houses?'

Unable to see why it should worry her, he nodded.

'I gather it's the one Maggie and Phil left,' he explained. 'It's actually two flats which is perfect for me as Juanita, my housekeeper-nanny, likes her own accommodation. She says she's not my wife or mother and is entitled to her own space.'

He can't be living in Maggie and Phil's place! The wailing words raced through Kate's brain, but she knew someone was—she'd seen a removal van there yesterday and wondered who could afford to pay for one on a Sunday.

She could move! It didn't matter that she'd decided she had to face her ghosts. She could do that next year, or the year after. She'd had good tenants in the house before, and the renovations she wanted to do could wait.

Except that she'd already stripped the wallpaper off most of the living room walls—

'Are you all right?'

The last word, with its rolled *r* only made her mad, panicky reaction worse, but she steeled herself to calm down. It was the man's accent, that was all, the deep Scottish voice would make anyone shiver.

That and the shadows in his dark eyes.

'I was thinking of coincidences,' she said, aware of the lameness of this excuse. 'I live next door.'

'Next door towards the hospital?' His eyebrows rose as he asked the question, and there was a puzzled look on his face, much like the one he'd worn when he'd asked her about her marital status—puzzled and a bit amused at the same time, though once again his eyes weren't smiling.

'Next door the other way,' she corrected, then before he could make some polite remark about the state of her overgrown garden or the junk from the living room she'd been depositing in the front yard, she added, 'It was my family home but it's been rented out for the past few years. I'm doing a bit of renovating now that I've moved back in.'

She didn't add, *With the ghosts*, although that was how it felt—just herself and the lonely ghosts in a house made for families, a house that should ring with children's laughter. Her mind flashed back to that day when she was eleven, staying with her friend Beth and visiting Beth's grandmother's house for the seemingly old lady's sixtieth birthday. *That* house had been filled with laughter while the children, all related in some way—connected and secure in the connections—had dashed around like restless puppies. This is a family, Kate had realised. *This* is what I want!

She shut the door on that memory, and fast-forwarded to years later and her adamant refusal to have a termination when Brian had suggested it. The baby would have been her family—*would have been*. She continued on her way. By now they were halfway across the corner of the park, and a short detour to the right took them to the road opposite Scoozi.

'That's the café,' she said, pointing to a place

that had seen so much drama played out among hospital personnel, the walls were probably impregnated with emotion.

In order to avoid any further asinine confessions, once they had coffee and carrot cake, which happened to be the cake of the day, in front of them, Kate introduced work topics, asking him why TGAs had become something of a specialty with him.

Serious, dark brown eyes studied her across the table and for a moment she thought he might not answer her question, but apparently he was only mustering his thoughts—not coming out with the first thing that came into his head, as she was wont to do!

'My first operation—the first I did as lead surgeon in a team—was a TGA and things went wrong. The coronary arteries were twisted around the heart, one of them going through the heart walls, and although we got there in the end, it was enough to make me realise that TGAs weren't the piece of cake I'd been considering them.'

Kate nodded, picturing the subdued panic in the

theatre as the team fought to sort out the problems that tiny heart would have presented.

'So you made a speciality of them?'

He smiled at her, a slow, lazy smile that made her stomach flip. Mouldy bread or something far more serious?

'Well, I did a lot more study into previous TGA cases and the complications the team could encounter during the operation, and tried to work out the best way of handling them.'

'Including coping with coronary arteries that wound through the heart wall?' Kate teased, unable to stop herself smiling at this stranger.

Not that he'd be a stranger for long, because they were neighbours, as well as colleagues. The thought caused another quiver in her abdomen, although she knew they'd only be friends. A man as good-looking as Angus McDowell could have his pick of women—should he want a woman—and scraggly redheads were unlikely to be on the top of his list.

'Including—in fact, especially—that,' he was

saying. 'Now, you're doing me a favour, showing me around, so I'll pay for our coffee.'

He stood and walked towards the till, leaving Kate wondering what she'd said that had caused such an abrupt departure.

And such a shift in mood, which had been becoming, well, neighbourly!

Angus knew he'd spoken curtly, not to mention practically knocking over his chair in his haste to get away from the table, but the redhead's smile—talking about coronary arteries of all things—had caused a physical reaction in his body, one he hadn't felt in a long time, and didn't want to dwell on now.

Jet lag might explain it.

Or concern about Hamish's rash.

Hamish...

Better to think about Kate's smile than the little boy he loved but knew he wasn't bonding with the way he should—the little boy who was the image of his mother.…

He paid for the coffees, but thinking of Kate's smile had him wondering if he could politely ask directions to the supermarket so they could part company and he could sort out what was happening to him.

Hardly!

Nor was he going to be able to avoid her in the future, given they'd be working on the same team—working closely.

Kate took him to the local shopping mall, within walking distance, and pointed out the best places to shop for meat and fruit.

'Stupid of me not to have thought of getting the car before we came here. Do you have a car?' Although she needed to shop herself—fresh bread for one thing—she was too eager to get out of his company to do it now, so added quickly, 'All the shops deliver, or you could get a cab. Will you be all right?'

Angus was forced to look at her now, although since the smile he'd been avoiding eye contact. The neat-fetured face was turned towards him and it seemed to him there was a shadow of anxiety in her pale green eyes.

For him?

Surely not! He was a grown man and quite capable of shopping and getting a cab home.

But it could hardly be for herself.

'Thank you, yes, of course I'll manage,' he responded, but at the same time, contrary now, he wished she'd stay—shop with him, share the cab, maybe come in and meet Hamish and Juanita—neighbourly...

'Stop kidding yourself,' he muttered under his breath when, goodbyes said, he was striding down the refrigerator aisle in the supermarket. 'One silly little smile across a coffee table and suddenly you're attracted to the woman!'

Not that anything could happen! It was Sod's Law once again. The one woman in the world he'd felt a physical response to in four years and she wanted children.

Well, she wanted to be a grandmother....

Why?

He recalled a depth of emotion in her voice and guessed the grandmother thing might be a cover for something else.

He shoved yoghurt and butter into his trolley,

then had to go back for cheese, knowing it wasn't quite true about the physical attraction. There'd been a couple of women but nothing serious, nothing he'd wanted to pursue.

So maybe an affair with this woman...

What *was* he thinking! He'd barely met her, didn't know her at all, and just because she looked like one of his mother's figurines, it didn't mean he had to go loopy over her. Besides, there were a whole raft of reasons why he shouldn't get involved. The effect it would have on his relationship—what there was of it—with Hamish for one. Two, she was a colleague. And three, well, he wasn't certain about three, although he knew there must be a three—didn't things always come in threes...?

Having worked the previous weekend, Kate had what was left of Monday off, but given the proximity of their houses and not wanting to run into Angus McDowell again, she chose instead to go back to work. There was always book work to be done, and reports to write up—work she was usually happy to ignore until the last possible moment.

It was almost dusk when she finally walked down the road to her house, dawdling until she reached the place where Angus McDowell now lived, then hurrying, looking busy, in case he happened to see her. But once past the boundary fence, she paused and surveyed the mess in her front yard. She should have hired a skip before she began moving the old furniture. She could have thrown things straight into it.

'It's a terrible mess.' The young, accusatory voice came from somewhere behind an old yellow sofa and the rolled *r*'s told her it must be the four-year-old from next door.

'It is indeed,' she agreed, walking towards the sofa and peering over the back to see the little boy with wide blue eyes beneath a tousled thatch of white-blond hair, crouched there, a tunnel through the hedge behind him revealing his access from the neighbouring yard. 'Does your dad know you're here?'

'He's out...' It sounded like 'oot' to Kate, who

had to smile, though if the child had been living in the U.S., surely his accent should be American rather than Scottish.

'And Juanita told me to get out from under her feet,' the small explorer finished. 'I was looking for an adventure. Me and McTavish—he's my dog but right now he's quantined—we like adventures.'

Kate nodded. She'd liked adventures herself when she'd been four. Unexpected pain hit her as memories of Susie's death flashed before her eyes. They'd shifted to this house soon after and here the family had fallen apart....

'Adventures can be fun but you need to be careful where you have them,' she told him. 'Perhaps you and McTavish, when he's back with you, should have your adventures in my backyard. Come on, I'll show you.'

She opened the side gate and led the way around her house, pushing through the branching arms of the untrimmed camellia hedge, to where the bushes grew even more thickly in the backyard, although there were patches of rather dry lawn here and there.

'See, you can come through the hedge here—' she pointed out another little tunnel '—and play safely. With the gate shut, McTavish won't be able to run on the road.'

'Hamish!'

The thunderous roar startled both of them, but Kate was first to respond.

'He's here, in my backyard. You won't fit through the tunnel so you'll have to come around the side.'

There was some muttering from the other side of the hedge, then the sound of next door's side gate opening.

Hamish, meanwhile, had read the situation well and disappeared through the hole in the hedge, back into his own yard and was even now calling out to Juanita, so when a scowling Angus McDowell appeared, Kate was the only one in his sights.

'Didn't you think to check that someone knew where he was?' he demanded. 'Surely if you've been involved with the childcare centre you've some notion of children's behaviour! We're going demented in there, looking for him and you're here chatting to him in your own backyard.'

There was more than anger in his eyes, there was fear, as well, but his tone had tightened Kate's nerves and she was in no mood to be conciliatory.

'Well, I'd hardly be chatting to him in your backyard, now would I?' she demanded. 'You were "oot," he told me, and Juanita sent him to play. As it happens, I found him in my front yard, and because there's only a low brick fence that a crawling infant could get over, and a front gate that doesn't shut properly, I brought him around the back to suggest if he goes adventuring he should use the backyard.'

She considered setting her hands on her hips and giving him a good glare but the shadows she saw again in his eyes had killed her anger. This man had suffered pain. Was still suffering it? Was his move to Australia part of a healing process?

It's none of your business, her head warned, but

having known pain—strong emotional pain—she couldn't help but wonder.

'Adventures! It's all he thinks about,' Angus muttered, still angry in the aftermath of anxiety but not seething any more. 'Some fool gave him a book that has a story about a boy and his dog that go on adventures and he's been mad for them ever since.'

He looked at the woman he'd been yelling at only minutes earlier and caught a hint of a smile she'd tried to hide.

'It isn't funny,' he snapped, not sure it was the smile or his reaction to it that had riled him.

She looked up at him, really smiling this time.

'It's a little bit funny,' she pointed out. 'Four years old and he's trespassing on my property and telling me it's a terrible mess. I'm sorry I didn't call out to Juanita to tell her he was with me, but it was a matter of a minute or two to show him the backyard where I knew he'd be safe. Take a look—could you get a better place for an adventure? And wouldn't you be more worried about him if he wasn't off having adventures? If he did nothing but sit around in front of the television all day?'

Angus sighed. Of course he'd be worried if Hamish wasn't always pushing himself to see more, do more, learn more. But did he want to admit it to this woman?

'I guess so,' he said, although reluctantly, 'and I know he misses the dog. Apparently we can visit him in quarantine but I haven't sorted out a vehicle yet so can't get to the quarantine station.'

'Well, that's easily fixed,' his neighbour replied. 'I'm on call at the weekend, so feel free to take my car. I've got a sat nav you can use so you won't get lost.'

Angus stared at her. Every cell in his body told him not to get more involved with this woman, but she wasn't inviting him to dinner, nor showing any signs she felt the slightest interest in him as a man; she was simply being neighbourly.

So why was he so hesitant to accept her offer?

'Or not,' she added with a shrug that showed little concern over his rudeness in not replying.

'Now, I've got to get inside, I've some stripping to do.'

Stripping?

It *had* to be jet lag that had his imagination working overtime, seeing that slight body slowly revealed as she eased off her clothes!

She started towards the back of the house, pausing to remove a key from under a lichen-covered Buddha, then as she straightened she turned back towards where he still stood, puzzled and disturbed, in her backyard.

'I've just remembered,' she said, 'there's a gate down the back between the two properties. Dad let the hedge grow over it when the house you're in was sold for rentals years ago, but if you hack away at the hedge and free the gate, Juanita will be able to get in here more easily if she needs to find the adventurers.'

'That's the first place burglars would look for a spare key,' he muttered, ignoring her advice about gates and hedges but finally getting his legs to work and moving towards her rather than the side gate.

Now she laughed.

'No way. They look under the doormat first, then under the flowerpots—look at all of them.' She waved her hands towards the mass of flowerpots clustered on mossy paving stones around the back door.

Angus *did* look. Looking at pot plants was infinitely preferable to the mental image lingering unwanted in his head.

Although she couldn't have meant that kind of stripping...

He turned more of his attention to the pot plants—a lot more.

'Herbs? I thought you said you couldn't cook. Why all the herbs?'

'I can cook, I just can't bake. When it comes to things like cakes and biscuits—I'm hopeless at those.'

It was one of the most inane conversations Kate had ever been involved in, but somehow she couldn't move away from the man who was now examining her herbs with an almost professional interest.

Or what seemed like one!

Why hadn't he left?

Why walk towards her rather than the side gate?

Surely the strangeness she was feeling in his presence wasn't reciprocated? Not just attraction as in physical awareness but attraction like iron filings to a magnet—a kind of inexorable pull....

'I've got a wall to strip and someone's calling you,' she said as a shrill, 'Daddy' wafted across the hedge.

'Yes,' he said, but still he didn't move, except to straighten up from his examination of the herbs and look directly at her, the shadows in his eyes not visible in the gathering dusk, so he was just a tall, dark and very handsome man!

'Yes,' he said again, then finally he turned away, calling back to Hamish, telling him he was coming, and disappearing around the side of the house.

Weird!

CHAPTER TWO

KATE left early for the hospital, telling herself it had nothing to do with not wanting to accidentally run into her neighbour and so having to walk with him. But maybe he'd had the same idea of avoiding her, or he always arrived at work an hour early, for he was the first person she saw as she entered the unit.

'The baby being transferred has arrived,' he said, a slight frown furrowing his brow.

'Bigger problem than you thought?' she asked, sticking to professionalism mainly because the toast she'd had that morning hadn't been made from mouldy bread but her stomach was still unsettled.

'No, the scans show really good coronaries, as far as you can ever tell from scans, but he hasn't got a name.'

Now Kate found herself frowning also.

'Hasn't got a name?' she repeated. 'But that's ridiculous. Of course he must have a name.'

'Baby Stamford,' Angus replied, his frown deepening.

'Oh, dear,' Kate muttered, hoping the first thing that had entered her head was the wrong one. 'But sometimes parents wait until their baby's born to name him or her, thinking they'll know a name that suits once they've seen the baby.'

Now Angus smiled, but it was a poor effort, telling Kate he knew as well as she did that sometimes the shock of having a baby with a problem affected the parents so badly they didn't want to give the child a name—didn't want to personalise the infant—in case he or she didn't survive.

Her heart ached for them, but aching hearts didn't fix babies.

'You're operating this morning?' she asked Angus.

He nodded.

'Good! That gives me an excuse to speak to the

parents, to explain what my part will be, before, during and after.'

She looked up at him.

'Shall we go together? A double act?'

Angus studied her for a moment, almost as if he was trying to place her in his life, then he nodded.

'The mother came by air ambulance with the baby, and the husband is driving down. Somewhere called Port something, I think they come from.'

'Port Macquarie,' Kate told him, 'and as far as I'm concerned, that's in our favour, the mother being here on her own. We might find out more from her than we would from the two together.'

'I prefer to speak to both parents,' Angus said in the kind of voice that suggested he was coolly pro-fessional in his approach to his job, not someone who got involved with the parents of the infants on whom he operated.

Which was fine, Kate admitted to herself as they walked down the corridor towards the parents' waiting room. A lot of paediatric surgeons were that way, finding a certain detachment necessary in a job that carried huge emotional burdens.

Although he was a single father himself—wouldn't that make him more empathetic?

And why, pray tell, was she even thinking about his approach to his job when it was none of her business? All she needed to know was that he was a top surgeon!

The waiting room was empty.

'The baby was born by Caesarean, so the mother is still a patient,' Becky, the unit secretary, told them. 'She's one floor up, C Ward, room fifteen.'

'Let's take the stairs,' Kate suggested, and when Angus grimaced she added, 'Not keen on incidental exercise? Don't you know that even the smallest amount of exercise every day can help keep you healthy?'

Far better to be talking exercise than thinking about empathy....

'I lived in America for five years, where everyone drives, and already today I've walked to work—incidental exercise, but mainly because I don't have a car.'

'You lived there for five years?' Kate queried, taking the second flight two steps at a time, only partly for the exercise. 'Yet Hamish has a broad Scots accent?'

Angus caught up with her as she opened the door.

'When my wife died, my mother came out to mind the baby, then my father took early retirement, so he and my mother were Hamish's prime carers when he learned to talk. They stayed until Hamish was three, then found Juanita for me before they returned to Scotland, where my father's old firm was only too happy to have him return to work.'

When his wife *died*?

There were plenty of single parents around, but most of them didn't have partners who had *died*!

No wonder he had shadows in his eyes.…

Kate tried to make sense of this—*and* make sense of why a casual answer to her question was having such an impact on her—as she led the way to C Ward, but once inside room fifteen, Angus's marital state was the last thing on her mind.

'I really don't care what you do,' the woman in the bed in room fifteen announced when they'd introduced themselves and explained the reason for their visit. 'This is just not the kind of thing that happens to people like us. I mean, my husband has his own business and I'm a barrister—we're both healthy, and we run in marathons. I keep telling people that the babies must have been mixed up. I held my baby when he was born and there was nothing wrong with him, and then suddenly people are saying his heart's not right and flying me off to Sydney, even refusing to take my husband in the plane.'

The tirade left Kate so saddened she was speechless, but thankfully Angus was there. He sat down carefully by the side of the bed, and spoke quietly but firmly.

'Mrs Stamford, I realise this is a terrible shock to you, but with this defect babies always seem perfectly healthy at first. It's only when a little duct between the two arteries starts to close and oxygenated blood keeps circulating through the lungs rather than around the body that a blueness is noticed, usually in the nail beds and lips of the infant.'

Kate saw the woman's fury mount, and expected further claims of baby-swapping, but to Kate's surprise, Mrs Stamford's anger was directed at Angus's choice of words.

'Defect? You're saying my baby has a defect?'

Time to step in before she became hysterical, Kate decided.

'It's fixable, the problem he has,' she said gently. 'That's why we're here. We need to explain the operation to you and get your permission to perform it.'

'And if I refuse?'

Oh, hell! Kate tried to think, but once again Angus took over.

'There could well be legal precedents that would allow us to operate anyway,' he said. 'I'm new to Australia but in many of the states in the U.S.—'

'Well, I very much doubt that,' Mrs Stamford interrupted him, although she seemed to have calmed down somewhat. Kate sought to reassure the woman.

'It's an operation that's frequently performed, and with excellent results,' she told her, 'and we're lucky to have Dr McDowell here as he specialises in it.'

She looked at Angus, expecting him to begin his explanation, but he hesitated for a moment before taking a small notebook and pen out of his shirt pocket.

'This might explain it best,' he said to Mrs Stamford.

Kate wondered about the hesitation—was it to do with the detachment she'd sensed earlier?—although now he was drawing a small heart on a clean page of the notebook, carefully inking in the coronary arteries which clasped the heart like protective fingers, then showing the two major arteries coming out the top of the organ.

'These coronary arteries which feed oxygenated blood to the heart muscle to keep it beating come off the aorta, the bigger of the two arteries coming out of the heart. The aorta is supposed to come out of the left ventricle while the pulmonary artery that divides in two and goes into the lungs comes out of the right. On rare occasions these two arteries are transposed and the aorta comes out of the right ventricle, with the pulmonary artery coming out of the left.'

Mrs Stamford was at least interested enough to look at Angus's drawing, and as she was quiet, he continued.

'What we have to do is first move the two coronary arteries, then we swap the major arteries, cutting the aorta and fixing it to the pulmonary artery where it comes out of the heart, and stitching the pulmonary artery to the aorta so the two arteries are now doing the jobs they're supposed to be doing.'

'For ever?' Mrs Stamford demanded.

Angus hid a sigh. She was right to ask, and had every right to know the truth, but this was one of the reasons he hated getting too involved with parents, having to tell them that the future could hold more operations, having to tell them that, although their child could lead a normal life, there was no guarantee of a permanent fix. Every conversation led to more emotional involvement—and often more pain for the parents.

'There's a chance the baby will need another operation when he's older.' He spoke calmly and dispassionately—straight medical information. 'The valves on the pulmonary artery are smaller than the aorta's valves and as these valves are left in place they might sometimes need to be expanded.'

'Leave the diagram,' Mrs Stamford said. Ordered? 'I'll speak to my husband and then talk to you again.'

She was dismissing them, and Kate waited while Angus pulled the page from his notebook, then they both left the room.

'*Is* there a legal precedent in some places to go ahead without permission?' Kate asked him.

'I've no idea,' he replied, 'but the woman was getting hysterical and I thought, as she's a barrister, legal talk might calm her down.'

'I think she's entitled to a *little* hysteria,' Kate muttered, wondering if Angus could really be as detached as he appeared.

She shrugged her shoulders, trying to ease the tension that had coiled in her body.

'It must be terrible for the parents,' she reminded him, 'to learn that there's something wrong with their child.'

Worse than losing an unborn child?

She thrust the thought away and turned her attention to what Angus was saying.

'Particularly parents who are barristers and run marathons?' he queried, the dryness in his voice suggesting he hadn't taken to Mrs Stamford, not one little bit. 'I wonder who she thinks *do* have children with heart defects? Common people like doctors and teachers? People who don't run marathons? I'm glad the baby is our patient, not the mother.'

'That's if the baby *is* our patient,' Kate reminded him, although she was wondering why Angus had chosen this specialty if he didn't like dealing with parents. Surely that was as important as successfully completing a delicate operation? Or nearly as important…

'He will be,' Angus assured her, moving to avoid a passer-by and accidentally bumping against her shoulder. 'I doubt any mother would deny her child a chance at life.'

'I hope you're right!' Kate murmured, though fear for the tiny scrap of humanity fighting for his life right now made her feel cold and shivery.

Except for a patch of skin on her shoulder which was very, very hot!

'Do you want to read his file? A paediatrician in the hospital where he was born gave him prostaglandin to keep the ductus arteriosus open and opened a hole between the atria to mix the oxygenated blood as much as possible but it won't hold him for long.'

Kate sighed.

'No, I'll read the file later. Right now I should go back in and talk to her.'

'Better you than me,' Angus said, although even as he spoke he felt saddened by his reaction and wondered just when he'd lost the empathy he used to feel with parents.

Fool! No need to wonder when he knew the answer. It was back when Jenna died—

'You make it sound as if I'm walking into an execution chamber,' Kate teased, jerking him out of the past. He found himself wishing she wouldn't do it—wouldn't talk to him so casually, as if they were old friends, and smile at the same time. It was affecting him in a way he didn't understand and certainly didn't want to consider. He didn't *do* emotion! Not any more....

'I didn't mean it that way,' he told her.

'No?'

Again the teasing smile, and again he felt a physical reaction to it, but before he could analyse it, Kate was speaking again.

'I can understand her anguish. Not only fear for her little son, but that terrible "why me" feeling she must be experiencing.'

'"Why me"?' Angus repeated, then he shook his head as he admitted, 'You're right. There's always a lot of "why me" isn't there?'

He looked unhappy and Kate realised that's exactly what he must have thought when his wife had died, as he tried to cope with his own grief and anguish, not to mention his son's loss of a mother.

And she, Kate, foolish woman that she was, had caused him pain by bringing it up!

But the 'why me' feeling was familiar to her, and although she wouldn't—couldn't—think about the really bad times she'd felt that way, maybe a couple of her less traumatic 'why me's' would cheer him up, chase the shadows from his eyes if only for a few minutes.

And lighten the atmosphere before she went back in to see Mrs Stamford!

'For my part they've been totally minor.' That was a lie but he'd never know. 'Things like a date passing out in his soup in the most expensive restaurant in town—a diabetic coma not drunkenness—and as it was a first date, it wasn't entirely surprising the relationship came to nothing. Then there was the one and only time I was persuaded to try skydiving. I got caught up in a tree and it took five hours to get me down, with full television coverage of a local drama. I know these are very trivial things compared to what Mrs Stamford is going through, but they do give me just some inkling of her "this can't be happening to me" feelings.'

Angus smiled and Kate felt a little spurt of happiness that she'd been able to make him smile, but the happiness faded as she remembered the task she'd set herself. She returned to Mrs Stamford's room.

'I thought you might like someone to talk to,' she said, giving the woman a quick professional once-over and not liking the pale, haggard face and red-rimmed eyes. 'There are counsellors, of course, that we could bring to you, but they wouldn't know the ins and outs of the op the baby needs. If you want to talk it out I'm willing to sit here and listen.'

'You said you were a doctor,' Mrs Stamford muttered in accusing tones. 'Don't you have other duties, people waiting for your services? We keep reading about the waiting lists for operations in hospitals, yet you've got time to sit and chat.'

Kate bit back a defensive retort. The woman was in terrible emotional pain; she was entitled to lash out.

'My job this morning was to prepare your baby for surgery,' Kate responded, speaking gently but firmly. 'As the anaesthetist I'm in charge of everything that goes into his blood and lungs until he goes onto the bypass machine, then afterwards until he's out of the post-op room. But I'm also a woman, and although I can't imagine the depth of the pain you're going through, I thought you might like a sounding board. Or to ask questions. Or just to have someone sitting with you for a while.'

Mrs Stamford's stiff upper lip did a little wobble, as did her lower lip, then she sniffed deeply as if to control tears that longed to flow.

'Will he die if he doesn't have the operation?' she asked, even paler now, if that was possible.

Kate hesitated.

'We can keep him alive for a while, but because

most of the oxygenated blood is circulating back through his lungs and not getting to his heart and brain, the answer's yes. But we have kids that have had this op coming back to visit us years later, fine healthy young girls and boys.'

The only response was another sniff, although the way the woman was twisting her hands told of her terrible agitation.

Kate longed to help her but wasn't sure how.

Maybe...

'Have you thought what you'd have done if you'd known the baby had a problem early on in your pregnancy. Would you have had a termination?'

Now colour rose in Mrs Stamford's cheeks.

'You mean, an abortion? No, I'd never have done that. A life's a life—my husband and I both agree on that.'

But now the baby's here you'd let him die? Kate thought, but she couldn't say it. Nor could she understand Mrs Stamford's thinking now, until the woman sighed and said, 'You're right. Of course I can't let him die. It was the shock! Give me whatever I have to sign, then go ahead and operate.'

Kate had won, so why did she feel as if she'd lost?

Because things were never that easy!

'He could still die,' she said, even more gently than she'd spoken earlier. 'These operations are performed quite often and with great success, but with any operation at any age there's a risk. You understand that.'

'Scared you'll be sued if you don't dot all the *i*'s and cross all the *t*'s?' Mrs Stamford snapped, but Kate heard the pain in her voice and knew the woman was close to breaking.

'I'm more afraid that having given permission if something does happen you'll blame yourself,' she said. 'You're already doing that, aren't you? Somehow you've convinced yourself this is all your fault, but congenital abnormalities can happen anywhere, any time.'

She stood up and moved closer to Mrs Stamford, putting her arms around her and holding her as the woman wept and wept.

'This is the damn problem with only having units like this in the capital cities,' Kate ranted to Angus a little later, the signed permission form in her hand. 'The patient, and usually the mother, are whisked away and end up miles from family support. She's got no-one, that woman, until her husband gets here. I know we can't have units like this in every hospital in Australia, but there should be a better way of doing things.'

Angus gave her shoulder a comforting pat, the physical effect of which jolted her out of her worry over Mrs Stamford's isolation, especially as she'd written her colleague down as a man who remained detached—too detached, she'd thought, for comforting pats!

'She's got the baby,' he reminded her, and Kate looked up at him.

'You mean...?'

'You've already achieved one miracle this morning,' Angus told her, 'so why not go for two. Go back in there and ask her if she'd like to go with him as he's wheeled to Theatre. We can get a wheelchair and she could touch him, hold his hand. Although if she doesn't want to bond with him in case he doesn't live—'

'She *thinks* she doesn't want to bond with him.'

Kate interrupted his objection, excited now by the idea. 'But maybe she's changed her mind about that, as well.'

She'd sounded positive about it, but deep inside she had her doubts, even wondered if it was wise to push Mrs Stamford this little bit more. But Angus seemed to think it was a good idea and he was looking far happier now than he had been earlier, so the least Kate could do was try.

She returned to the room where Mrs Stamford was lying back against the pillows, her eyes closed and only a little more colour in her face than when Kate had first seen her.

'We'll be taking him to Theatre very soon, and I wondered if we arranged a wheelchair for you and a wardsman to push it, you'd like to come up to the PICU and go as far as the theatre with him.'

Mrs Stamford's eyelids lifted and dark brown eyes stared fiercely at Kate.

'What are you? Some kind of avenging angel, determined to push me further and further?'

'I just wondered,' Kate said lamely, 'seeing as

you're here on your own until your husband arrives and he, the baby, is on his own, as well. Maybe you could support each other.'

Oh, boy! Wrong thing to say! Mrs Stamford was in tears again, flooding tears and great gulping sobs.

Kate held her again, and it was only because she was holding her, she heard the whispered instructions.

'Get the bloody wheelchair, but I want a nurse not a wardsman wheeling me. Men don't understand.'

Uh-oh! Was it Mr Stamford, not Mrs Stamford, who'd found it hard to accept a less-than-perfect child? Had she consulted him—phoned him—before she signed the permission-to-operate paper?

And while Kate could have argued that some men were far more understanding and supportive than some women, she held her tongue. She gave Mrs Stamford a final hug and darted off, not wanting to give the woman time to change her mind. She arranged the transportation, then raced back up to the floor above, knowing she had to be there to intubate Baby Stamford and prepare him for his lifesaving op.

'So tiny, the veins.'

She didn't have to glance up to know it was Angus hovering beside her in the treatment room as she put a peripheral line into the baby's foot, already having secured one in his jugular and administered the first mild sedative.

'So tiny we need to work out better ways of doing this—smaller, more flexible catheters. You'd think it would be easy but I've been working with technicians from one of the manufacturing companies for over a year now, and we're no further advanced. Too fine and they block, or twist or kink—it's so frustrating!'

Angus studied the back of her head—a coloured scarf now hiding the bright hair—as she concentrated fully on her task.

She'd been working with techies to improve catheters? Kate Armstrong was full of surprises, not least of which had been the way she'd talked

Mrs Stamford out of her indignation and allowed the woman's natural maternal instincts to come out.

The redhead's body brushed against his as she straightened up and *his* body went into immediate response mode. Not good where Kate Armstrong was concerned. She wanted kids—well, grand-kids, which meant, as she'd pointed out, having kids first.

She was not for him!

Even though the 'grandmother' thing intrigued him! Not to mention whatever lay behind it….

Was it because of the familiar noises in the oper-ating theatre, the sizzle of the bovie as it cut and cauterised tiny vessels, the bleeps of the monitors as they kept Kate up-to-date on Baby Stamford's condition, the subdued chatter of the staff, the music playing in the background, that Angus felt so at home? Although this was not only his first operation at Jimmie's but the first time he'd worked with any of the team.

Oliver Rankin was assisting. He was quiet, neat

and efficient, although Angus rather thought he was casting glances in Kate's direction a little too often. Clare Jackson was operating the bypass machine, waiting for the order to use it to take over the work of Baby Stamford's tiny heart. Clare Jackson might not want children, Angus thought, standing back so Oliver could lift the pericardium away from Baby Stamford's heart.

The thought startled him, and he shut it down immediately, dismayed to find himself, for the first time in years, thinking of something other than the operation while in Theatre. He prided himself on his total concentration on the job, and although he often joined in the general chat and jokes, his mind never strayed far from the tiny patient on the table.

She was far better looking, beautiful, in fact— Clare Jackson—so why was he, too, glancing up at Kate from time to time.

Because she's the anaesthetist, of course, and she's the one who knows how the baby's doing, down there, all but hidden with the cage to protect his head and wrappings covering all his little body except his chest.

'Blood gases fine,' the woman he was trying to block from his mind said. 'Heartbeats 130 a minute.'

With the little heart fully exposed, Angus inserted cannulas into the aorta and an atrial vein; Oliver attached the tubes that would put Baby Stamford on bypass—the tubes connecting to the machine which would oxygenate his blood and pump it through his body.

'Pressure's up,' Kate said, reassuring everyone, although Clare was now controlling what happened to the baby's blood pressure.

'Check blood gases and start cooling him.' Angus gave the order, one hundred percent of his attention back on his patient, the information coming in from Kate and Clare clicking computerlike into his brain, his mind whirling as he worked, total concentration on what he was doing but thinking ahead, always anticipating any problem, at the same time.

'Why do we cool them?' the circulating nurse

asked, her voice suggesting she'd often wondered but for some reason had never wanted to ask.

'It cuts down the risk of organ damage when the flow of blood to the brain and other major organs stops—when we stop the heart to do the repair.'

Oliver explained, while Angus inserted a tiny tube into the aorta, where it was rising out of the heart. Through this he'd put the poison that would stop the heart beating and, once that went in, it was a matter of timing every second of the operation.

Kate watched him at work, waiting patiently until all the blood drained from Baby Stamford's heart, then switching the coronary arteries so neatly and quickly she didn't realise they were done until he stood and stretched.

Once straightened, he looked across at her, and she nodded and held up a thumb, but there'd been something in his dark eyes that had suggested he was looking at *her*, not at the anaesthetist. Ridiculous, of course, but she shivered in spite of herself, then turned all of her attention back to the patient on the table and the machines that told her what was happening.

Less than an hour later the baby's heart was beating on its own, the little hole in his heart repaired, the arteries switched so they would now do the jobs they were intended to do. And though Angus had left a pacemaker in Baby Stamford's chest to keep his heart rate stable, and various drainage tubes and measuring devices were still attached to him, he was doing well.

Kate had to smile as she accompanied her tiny comatose patient to the intensive-care room. He would be her responsibility until he regained consciousness, although Clare was in charge of the machine that was keeping him breathing.

'Getting him off the ventilator is the next hurdle,' Clare, who was walking beside Kate, said.

'Only if he needs it for a long time, but he's come through very well—all his blood values were good,' Kate replied, and Clare smiled.

'You're a glass-half-full person, right?' she said.

Was she?

'I've never thought about it,' Kate admitted honestly.

'Never thought about what?' a deep voice asked, and she turned to see Angus had joined them in the small room.

'Whether I'm a pessimist or an optimist,' she said, thinking of the times when sadness and loss had threatened to overwhelm her and whether that was pessimism.

'Oh, definitely an optimist, I'd say,' Angus told her, almost smiling, almost teasing. 'What else would you call a woman who organised childcare for children she doesn't yet have?'

'You what?' Clare demanded, but Kate silenced Angus with a 'don't you dare' look.

Bad enough she'd admitted her grandmother obsession to one person without the entire hospital knowing it.

'What about you, Angus,' she asked to divert the conversation. 'Are you a glass-half-full or a glass-half-empty person?'

He studied her for a moment.

'You know, I've never thought about it. Definitely

half full as far as patients are concerned. I could never do an operation if I doubted I'd be improving a child's quality of life.'

'You've children yourself?' Clare asked, and Kate felt a surge of something that couldn't possibly be jealousy flood through her veins at the other woman's interest.

'One, Hamish—he's four,' Angus answered, while Kate wondered why Alex couldn't have found a less beautiful perfusionist.

'Probably ready for a little sister or brother,' Clare suggested, and though Kate knew this was just idle talk as they all watched the monitors that told them Baby Stamford was doing well, she resented the other woman's interest. Although Clare probably didn't know Angus was a widower.

'Not for Hamish, I'm afraid,' Angus replied. 'He's going to be an only child for life.'

Poor kid, Kate thought, but before she could point out the disadvantages—the haunting loneliness she'd felt as an only child—Clare was talking again, talking and smiling.

Flirting?

'Good for you!' she said. 'I'm one of four and the number of times I've wished I was an only child! You've no idea. Having to share toys, wearing hand-me-downs—not that we lived on bread and jam or the hand-me-downs were rags, but I think I was born to be an only child.'

Selfish! Kate muttered to herself, but there was something so open and honest about Clare that she found herself looking past the beauty to the woman within.

And liking her!

Damn!

Double damn if Angus were to fall for her, and why wouldn't he?

Not that it was any of Kate's business who he fell for, so why was she still thinking about Clare, thinking perhaps she was attached—*surely* she was attached; how could someone so beautiful be unattached?

'Look, there's no point in all three of us being here. Why don't you two grab a coffee break—in fact, it's past lunchtime. The canteen is good, and cheaper than the coffee shop on the ground floor. You know where to go?'

Was she pushing them together? Angus wondered. Then knew it was only because, for some indefinable reason, he was attracted to Kate Armstrong that he'd even consider she might be doing such a thing. This was work—two colleagues sharing lunch. He had to get his mind off Kate Armstrong and, having decided that, lunch with the beautiful Clare might be just what he needed.

Kate watched them depart, telling herself it was for the best, particularly now she'd heard Angus being so adamant about not producing siblings for Hamish. Given that fact, Angus McDowell was definitely not the man for her.

Not that he'd shown the slightest sign of wanting to be, so why she'd been idly fantasising about him she had no idea!

No idea apart from the attraction that had startled her body into life when she'd first met him. *Her* body, that was usually biddable and dependable and had rarely felt anything more than a lukewarm interest in any man since Brian and even he hadn't provoked much physical reaction.

Enough of attraction; she'd think about something else. Like why was Angus so definite about not wanting more children? Perhaps it was another way of saying he'd never marry again?

Get your mind back on work!

She checked Baby Stamford, wishing he had a name, then was surprised to hear the whirr of a wheelchair coming towards her. Mrs Stamford, pushed by a man who definitely wasn't a wardsman.

'They said he'd come through very well.' Mrs Stamford's voice was back in accusatory mode, daring Kate to argue this piece of good news.

'He's a little champion,' she assured the still-pale woman, then she held out her hand to the man. 'I'm Kate Armstrong, the anaesthetist. I'll be keeping an eye on him for the next few hours.'

'Pete Stamford,' the man responded, shaking Kate's hand, although all his attention was on his baby son who was so dwarfed by wires and tubes it was hard to see much of him. 'You keep a personal eye on him? Not just watch monitors?'

'I like to be here most of the time,' Kate told him, and was surprised when the man's face darkened.

'Then it's obvious to me he's not out of the woods yet,' he said, his muted voice still managing to convey anger.

'He's been through a huge ordeal for such a tiny baby,' Kate said gently. 'Being on bypass takes a lot out of them, and we stop his heart while the switch happens, poor wee mite, but there's no cause for anxiety. I stay because I like to watch until I'm certain he's over the effect of the anaesthetic and sleeping naturally. I can't always do it, because I've usually other ops scheduled, so today it's a bit of a treat for me.'

Pete Stamford eyed her with great suspicion and Kate was glad he hadn't come when all three of the specialists had been in the room. Then he would have been truly alarmed.

And she was even gladder—or should that be more glad, she wondered—when she realised that

Mrs Stamford had wheeled herself closer to the cot, put her hand through the vent and was softly stroking her baby's arm, talking quietly to him at the same time.

Kate felt her heart turn over at the sight, then realised Baby Stamford's father was also looking at his wife, while tears streamed down his cheeks.

Unable to resist offering comfort, Kate put her arm around his shoulders and he turned to her and sobbed, his chin resting on her head.

'It's okay,' she said, more or less to both of them. 'You've been through such an ordeal and it isn't over yet, but the worst part is behind him, so maybe, little champ that he is, he deserves a name.'

To Kate's surprise, Pete straightened. He stepped towards his wife, taking her hand as they both chorused, 'Bob.'

Bob?

They were going to call the baby Bob?

What about Jack and Tom and Sam, simple syllable names that were in vogue right now? What kind of a name for a baby was Bob?

It was Mrs Stamford who eventually explained.

'We had a dog once, a border collie, who was the most faithful animal God ever put on earth. Even when he was dying of some terrible liver disease, he would drag himself to the doorway to greet Pete every night, and every morning he'd bring in the paper and drop it at my feet, right up to the day he died. He had more strength and courage than any human we've ever known, so it seems right to name this little fellow after him.'

Now Mrs Stamford was crying, too, and Kate quietly backed out of the room, wanting to leave the pair of them to comfort each other—and to get to know their little son.

Bob!

Angus returned as she was standing by the main monitors in the PICU. He peered into the room where the couple were, then turned to Kate, his eyebrows raised.

'They're okay,' she told him. 'They've called him Bob.'

'Bob?' Angus repeated. 'Ah, after a grandfather no doubt.'

'After their old dog,' Kate corrected, then she laughed at the expression on Angus's face. 'Thinking how it would be to have a child called McTavish?' she teased, and although he smiled, once again the smile didn't reach his eyes.

'I meant it when I said earlier there'd be no more children in my family,' he said, and Kate sensed he was telling her something else.

Telling her he, too, felt an attraction between them but it couldn't be?

She was not sure, but her body seemed to take it that way, disappointment forming a heavy lump in her chest.

CHAPTER THREE

'His name's Pete—Mr Stamford, that is,' she said to Angus, anxious to get him out of her company. 'I'm sure he'd appreciate meeting you and talking to you about the op and Bob's expected progress.'

Her tongue stumbled over 'Bob,' and Angus smiled at her, restarting all the sensations she didn't want to feel. Surely if she ignored them they'd go away, and for all the fancy she'd had earlier, she doubted Angus would be attracted to her. Especially not with a beauty like Clare around.

Or perhaps he no longer felt attraction for anyone. Perhaps his adamant declaration that Hamish would be an only child was because he was still in love with his dead wife—that was a possibility.

In which case he should do something to dampen down *his* attractiveness, Kate thought gloomily.

He walked away and she looked through the window to where he stood, talking to Pete and Mrs Stamford, and though she couldn't hear what they were saying, in her imagination she heard his seductive accent and knew ignoring the manifestations of attraction would be difficult to do.

Perhaps an affair—

He's not interested in you!

One part of her head was yelling at the other part. She tried to remember back to lectures on the brain and which bits controlled what. She'd never been particularly interested in neurology and worked quite happily on the theory that half her brain did emotion while the other half did common sense. And while the common-sense half—maybe that part was more than half in her case—usually held sway, she knew once the emotion part was awoken, it could be difficult to ignore.

Double damn again.

'You talking to yourself?'

The nurse sitting at the monitor looked up and Kate realised she'd sworn aloud.

'Probably,' she told the nurse. 'Early dementia setting in.'

'Not surprising, the work you do, anaesthetising tiny babies. I couldn't do it. I find it hard enough to watch them on the monitor. I'm getting married next week and we want to have kids, but I'll have to transfer out of the PICU before I can even think about it. Pregnancy's scary enough without knowing all the things that could be going wrong with the baby!'

Kate watched the monitor and considered this. It was what she did, caring for babies during life-saving operations, so she'd always seen the work as positive, but as Angus and the Stamfords left Bob's room and she returned to it, she wondered if knowing the things that could happen would make pregnancy better or worse.

Better, surely, for there would be no unknowns.

But had she chosen it, subconsciously steered her career this way, because of the baby she'd lost?

No, that had been back in second year at university, before she'd begun her medical training, when medicine had still been only one of the options she'd been considering.

But her affinity for babies came from somewhere....

She shook her head, shaking away thoughts that had been safely locked in some dusty closet in her mind for many years.

'You handled Mrs Stamford very well. Are you able to feel that empathy for all your patients' parents?'

Angus appeared when Kate, some hours later, was in the surgeons' lounge checking the operating list for the following day, baby Bob now in Clare's care.

Kate turned towards him, but though looking at him usually produced a smile, this time it was forced.

'That's a strange question,' she told him, still puzzling over the man who'd asked it. 'I would think anyone would feel empathy for someone with a sick child.'

'Perhaps!' He shrugged off her assertion with that single word, as if to say *he* didn't, but she'd seen glimpses of an empathetic man behind the cool detachment he wore like a suit.

Or maybe armour?

'Not "perhaps" at all,' she argued. 'I bet you feel it or have felt it. In fact, I'd like to hazard a guess it's because of the children you see with problems that you've decided not to have more children.'

'You couldn't be more wrong.'

The blunt statement struck her like a slap and she felt the colour she hated rising in her cheeks. He must have seen it, for his next question was conciliatory, to say the least.

'But on that subject, you see these infants yourself, yet you still want to have children. Why's that?'

He'd asked the question to turn the conversation back on her, Kate knew that, but it was something she'd been thinking about since talking to the nurse earlier at the monitors. She'd locked the memory of her unborn child back into that dusty closet where it belonged, but the other issue was, and always had been, family.

How could she explain the loneliness she'd experienced as a child, and the ache for family, accentuated this time of year as Christmas drew near? Oh, she had friends who always welcomed her, but Christmas was for families, and since she was a child, she'd dreamed that one day she'd be the one cooking the turkey—she'd be the one with the children....

Pathetic, she knew, so she answered truthfully—well, partly truthfully.

'It's more a family thing,' she admitted. 'I was—I was an only child of parents who had no siblings living in Australia so I had no cousins or aunts or grandparents. Then one day—'

'When you were eleven,' he interrupted, and she nodded.

'—I was staying with a friend and we went to her grandmother's sixtieth birthday party and I saw a family in action and knew it was what I wanted.'

She kept her eyes on him as she spoke, daring him to laugh at her, wondering why the hell she was pouring out these things to a virtual stranger when she'd held them close inside her lonely heart for all these years!

He didn't laugh, but nor did he respond, the silence tautening between them.

'Besides,' she said, determined to get back to easy ground, 'why wouldn't I want to pass on the genetic inheritance of pale skin and red hair—so suitable to a hot Australian climate.'

Now he did respond, even smiling at the fun she was poking at herself.

'Ah, selective breeding. I do agree with that, but you could do that with one child—even be a grandmother with one child—so why children plural.'

Now Kate's smile was the real deal, and she shook her head as she replied.

'You're a persistent cuss, aren't you? We barely know each other and you're asking questions even my best friends don't ask. They just accept— Kate, yes, the one who wants kids. They usually emphasise the *want* and sigh and roll their eyes because they already have children and are often wondering why on earth they thought it was such a good idea.'

'Which gets you very neatly out of answering my question,' Angus said, but he didn't persist and Kate was happy to let the subject drop, as memories of her father's long illness and eventual death when her aloneness really struck home—no-one to share the caring, or share the pain and loss—came vividly to mind, bringing back the surging tide of grief she thought she'd conquered years ago.

Had her colleague seen something in her expression—a change of colour in her cheeks—that he held out his hand?

'Come on, baby Bob is fine, and we've a full day tomorrow. I'll walk you home.'

Kate considered arguing, making the excuse that she wanted to check the children on the next day's operating list, but weariness was seeping through her bones and, dodging the hand he'd offered to guide her through the door, she led the way into the corridor.

Why did she intrigue him? And why so suddenly was he attracted, he who didn't believe in instant attraction? Angus pondered this as they walked down the leafy street towards their houses. The summer sun was still hot, although it was late afternoon, and sweat prickled beneath his shirt, but that was nothing to the prickling in his skin when he saw this woman unexpectedly, or an image of her flicked across his inner eye.

'Does it get much hotter?' he asked, thinking an innocuous conversation about the weather would distract him from considering his reactions to his companion.

'Much,' she said cheerfully. 'It's only late November. Summer doesn't officially begin until December, and February can be a real killer, but at least you've got a nice olive skin. You can go to the beach to cool off and not risk turning as red as a lobster and coming out in freckles the size of dinner plates.'

'Dinner plates?' he queried, smiling, but more,

he feared, because she'd said he had nice skin than at her gross exaggeration.

'Well, very freckly,' she countered.

'Ah, the great genetic inheritance you want to pass on to your children!'

She sighed and ran a hand through her tangled red curls.

'I'm very healthy—surely that's important,' she pointed out.

It was a silly conversation but the children thing nagged at Angus. He could accept that it was natural for a woman to want children, but Kate's desire seemed slightly out of kilter—more like determination than desire.

And he was obsessing about this, why?

Because he was attracted to her, of course!

Stuff and nonsense, as his mother would say. It was jet lag, not attraction—attraction didn't happen this fast.

'Can Hamish swim? He'll need to learn if he can't. There are learn-to-swim classes for children in every suburb.'

Had Kate been talking the whole time he

muddled over attraction or had she just come out with this totally unrelated question?

Either way, he'd better answer her.

'*Need* to learn?' he repeated.

Her easy strides hesitated and she looked towards him.

'*I* think so! There are far too many drowning fatalities of small children in Australia each year. No matter what safety measures are put in place, and what warnings are issued, the statistics are appalling.'

Something in her voice sent a shiver down his spine and he hurried to reassure her.

'He *can* swim. Loves the water but has no fear, which is always a bit of a worry.'

She was standing looking at him, and he almost felt her shrugging off whatever it was that had bothered her earlier, although when he really looked at her, he saw the pain in her eyes.

'Someone you knew drowned?' he guessed, then regretted the casual question when all the colour left her face.

But she didn't flinch, tilting her chin so she could look him in the eyes.

'My sister—she was only two. It was a long time ago, but you don't forget.'

He reached out and touched her arm.

'I'm so sorry, I really am. I shouldn't have persisted.'

She rallied now, shrugging off the memories.

'That's okay, you weren't to know. Things happen. But you can understand why I'm a wee bit obsessive about children learning to swim.'

'Of course you are.' He squeezed her arm where he was holding it, feeling her bones beneath the flesh. 'Well, be assured Hamish will be fine in the water. We're quite near the beach, I believe.'

Her smile caught him by surprise, as did his gut's reaction to it.

'Quite near the beach? You really were thrown straight in the deep end,' she said. 'You haven't had time to work out your surroundings at all.'

Then, as if their previous conversation had never happened, she looked up at the sky, where the sun was heading slowly towards the west.

'With daylight saving, it'll still be light for a while. What if I pile you and Hamish and Juanita into my car and we do a quick tour of the neighbourhood. We can have a swim and finish with fish and chips at the beach—if Hamish is allowed to eat fish and chips.'

She was being neighbourly, possibly to banish memories his careless question had provoked, but the offer told him more about Kate Armstrong than she'd probably intended it to. She was the kind of person who would always put herself out for others. She'd had no need to go back into Mrs Stamford's room that morning, but had known the other woman was in deep emotional pain and had decided to make one more attempt to help her.

Now she was offering to drive his little family to the beach.

She *should* have children! A giving person like Kate would be a wonderful mother. Angus remembered a book he'd read on parenting that explained no matter how hard a father tried he could never fully replace a mother. Something to do with wiring…

If Hamish had a mother, would that let Angus off the hook? Allow him to feel less, not exactly guilty, but disquieted about his interaction with his son?

He shook his head as if to shake away the notion. He was fine as a father, spent time with Hamish, did whatever he could for him....

'Well?' Kate demanded, and Angus pulled himself together.

'We'd be delighted, and thanks to his early up-bringing Hamish loves fish and chips. It's practically a staple diet back home in Scotland.'

What was she doing? Was she mad, getting more involved with her neighbours instead of less? Kate left him at his gate and strode ahead, then found Hamish and a woman who must be Juanita sitting on her yellow sofa.

'I thought I told you the backyard was for adventures,' she scolded Hamish, although she softened the words with a smile.

'This isna an adventure,' he told her, four-year-old scorn scorching the words. 'I'm with Juanita. We're waiting for you to come home so I can—'

'Introduce me,' the woman said, standing and holding out her hand to Kate. 'I am Juanita Cortez.'

She was a solid, olive-skinned woman of about fifty, Kate guessed as she introduced herself, and asked Juanita how she was settling in.

'We are nearly there,' Juanita replied. 'Angus has sorted a kindergarten for Hamish and I've found an organisation for ex-pat Americans that meets once a month, and another place where I can go to play bridge, so I will soon meet plenty of people.'

'Well done you,' Kate responded, admiring the other woman's nous in getting organised, but she was watching Hamish as she spoke, watching Angus swing his son into the air before depositing him on his shoulders, normal father stuff but somehow Angus was never looking at the little boy.

Not directly.

Seeing them together, so unalike, Kate wondered if Hamish looked like his mother, and therefore was too painful a reminder....

Oh, dear!

'Come on,' Angus said, 'let's get changed. Kate's taking us to the beach.'

'Are you, Kate? Are you really?' the little boy perched on Angus's shoulders demanded.

Stupid, this is stupid getting more involved with them, but something in the anxious young eyes made her reply immediately.

'Of course. Get your swimmers, or whatever you Yanks and Scots call swimming costumes and meet me at the shed in my backyard in half an hour.' Kate turned back to Juanita. 'You'll join us.'

Juanita looked far less interested in a trip to the beach than Hamish had been.

'If you don't mind, I'd prefer to stay at home. I need to send some emails to my family to let them know we've arrived and are settling in, then I must make some phone calls about the ex-pat organisation and bridge club.'

As Angus and Hamish had disappeared into their house, Kate assumed this would be okay with him, so she nodded to Juanita and hurried inside herself, worrying again because a swim was just what she needed to wash away the tension of the day. But on the other hand, letting Angus McDowell see her lily-white body in a swimsuit, especially on a beach full of bronzed bathing beauties, was a very embarrassing idea.

As if he cared what she looked like in a swimming costume, the common-sense half of her brain told her, though the sensible admonition wasn't strong enough to stop a rather wistful sigh.

She changed into her swimming costume, pulled shorts and a T-shirt over it, then dug through the kitchen junk drawer in search of the car keys. She used the car so rarely, the keys got buried under spare change, receipts and reminder notices from the library—even an apple core, today, although how that had got in there, Kate had no idea.

Then out the back door, locking it, and casting a quick glance at her pots to check if they needed watering. Later—she'd do that later, because excited voices from the far end of her backyard told her Angus and Hamish had arrived.

'We came down the lane,' Angus explained,

'although I've found the gate between the properties. I just haven't had time to hack through the jungle to release it.'

It's because he's got this outer carapace of an easygoing man that I feel as if I've known him for ever, Kate decided as she unlocked the shed and turned on a light, revealing her father's ancient old car. But all he lets people see is the outside....

'That's your car?'

Two voices chorused the question, the younger one excited, the older one full of disbelief.

'It goes,' Kate said defensively.

'I think it's super,' Hamish announced. 'Like something out of a storybook. Has it got a name?'

As a person who thought giving names to inanimate objects was stupid, Kate longed to say no, but if she did, the car would probably hear her and refuse to start.

'My father called it Molly,' she admitted, hoping maybe Angus, who was walking around it, examining it the way one would an antique, hadn't heard, but just in case he hadn't, Hamish made sure he knew.

'Did you hear that, Dad? We're going for a ride in Molly.'

He was patting the car's pale blue paintwork, his little hands leaving prints in the dust, so Kate was squirming with embarrassment before she'd even opened the doors. She did that now, helping Hamish into the back seat, pulling down the booster seat and fastening the seatbelt around him, then getting in the car herself.

'Molly?' Angus queried softly as he slid into the passenger seat beside her.

'My father named her.' Defensive didn't begin to describe how Kate felt, until she remembered—'And if you want to borrow the car to visit your dog at the weekend, then I don't want to hear another comment, thank you.'

Before Angus could reply, Hamish began chattering about McTavish and how much he would like a car called Molly, and the child's innocent delight in the situation eased Kate's tension, so by the time they'd driven around the immediate neighbourhood and arrived at the beach at Coogee, she'd even stopped worrying about Angus seeing her in a swimming costume.

He'd have been better not having seen her in a swimming costume, Angus decided as their chauffeur slipped out of her shorts and shirt, revealing a pale but perfect body. All of his mother's figurines were decorously covered, so it wasn't a similarity to one of them that sent his heartbeat into overdrive.

It must be the prolonged period of celibacy his libido had been suffering. His last female friend had fallen out with him six months ago over the amount of time he spent with Hamish. The argument had been fierce, mainly because Angus knew he spent the time with Hamish in an attempt to make up for what he didn't give the child. Not love, exactly, for he loved him deeply, just... He didn't know what the 'just' was, except that it was there—a missing link.

But the outcome of that argument had been that he'd decided it was easier to stay out of relationships for a while, especially as by that time he'd been offered the job in Sydney and had known he'd be moving on.

So, have a swim and settle down, he told himself, shucking off his own shorts and polo shirt, then following his son and Kate down to where green waves curled, then broke into foaming swirls that slid quietly up the beach.

'These are big waves.' The awe in Hamish's voice made Kate smile. 'In Scotland we have little waves and in America there aren't any beaches.'

'Not where you lived,' Kate reminded him, forbearing to point out America had thousands of miles of coastline on two oceans. He was jumping the waves as they washed towards him, shrieking with glee, and Kate's heart ached with wanting. To have a child, her own child—any child, she was beginning to think.

Although it was a baby her arms ached for....

'Want to go out deeper?'

Angus scooped up his son and strode towards the curling waves.

Presumably Angus could swim.

Kate watched them go, the ache still there—

stronger if anything. It was all to do with family. Were Angus and Hamish a family? Was the base of family solid beneath the little boy? Had it not been solid in her case, even before Susie drowned? Had her family been doomed to disintegrate like so many families did these days, even before Susie died?

She could see the pair in the deeper water, ducking under waves, and remembered times, after her mother died, when she and her father had come to the beach. He would take her out into deep water and throw her over the waves. He'd loved her, Kate had no doubt of that, but it had been a detached, distracted kind of love, the kind one might give to a specially favoured pet, the concept of family perhaps as unfamiliar to him, another only child, as it was to Kate.

Enough! She dived beneath the next wave, surfaced for a breath, then dived again, coming up beyond the breakers, feeling the water wrap around her body, cooling and soothing her, reminding her of all the wonderful things in her life, counterbalancing the aches.

A good wave was coming, rising up above the others, curling early. Swimming hard she caught it and rode it to the beach, aware of passing Angus and Hamish on her way. She lay where the wave had left her on the sand until an excited little boy joined her.

'Will you teach me to do that, will you, Kate, will you?'

Kate rolled over and smiled up at him.

'I surely will, champ,' she said. 'Next time I'm at the shops I'll get you a little boogie board. It's easiest to practise on that in the shallows, then I can take you out in front of me on my bigger board. One day when you're older, if your Dad decides to stay in Sydney, you might learn to surf. See the people at the far end of the beach, standing up on their surfboards?'

'Can you do that? Can you teach me that?'

His excitement had him hopping up and down, splashing her with water.

'There are better teachers than me, for board surfing,' she told him, sitting up and looking around for Angus. Perhaps she *should* have asked if he could swim! Then his body, sleek as a seal's, slipped onto the beach beside her.

Angus sat up and shook the water from his hair.

'I didn't catch it way out where you did,' he said to the woman he'd been watching since she was deposited on the sand, a slim white mermaid in a green bathing suit. 'I just surfed the broken bit. It's been a long time since I caught a wave—student days at St Ives in England, an annual summer pilgrimage.'

He'd flopped onto the tail end of the wave to stop thinking about her, but now, this close, not thinking of her was impossible. The beautiful skin, so fine and pale he could see the blue veins in her temples, and in the slender lines of her neck, then the fiery red hair, darker now, wet and bedraggled, framing her face like a pre-Raphaelite painting.

'Kate is going to teach me how to ride on the waves,' Hamish announced, and now colour swept into her cheeks.

'I wasn't sure if you knew how. He asked me, but of course, you're a surfer, you can teach him.'

'Maybe we could both teach him.'

Angus heard the words come out and wished there was some way he could unsay them. How could he include someone else in his family before he'd made sure it *was* a family? It had obviously embarrassed her, as well, for the colour in her cheeks had darkened, and she stood and headed back into the water.

'I'll just catch another wave.' The words floated back over her shoulder before she dived beneath the breakers.

'Can I do that? Can I?' Hamish demanded, so Angus put thoughts of pale-skinned mermaids right out of his mind and concentrated on teaching his son to dive beneath the waves.

'Time for a shower and something to eat?'

Angus and Hamish, the diving lessons over, were sitting on the beach, making sandcastles, when the mermaid surfed right to their feet, lifting her head to ask the question.

'We can shower up on the esplanade,' she added, pointing towards the road, then, as if that was all the information he would need to realise the swim was over, she stood and walked back to where they'd left their towels and clothes. Angus hoisted Hamish onto his back and followed, thanking Kate as she picked up their clothes and handed them to him.

'There are changing rooms if you don't want to put your clothes on over your swimmers,' she said, 'but I find it's cooler to stay wet underneath, and as we can eat our fish and chips in the park, it doesn't really matter.'

Very matter-of-fact, yet that was what this outing was, a neighbourly gesture.

So why did he feel disappointed?

Feel as if something had changed between them?

For the worse!

She held their clothes while he showered with Hamish, then dried the little boy with her towel while Angus dried himself.

Being busy with Hamish meant Kate didn't have

to look at Angus's sleek, wet body. She'd always considered herself immune to hormonal surges of attraction but the man next door was definitely setting her hormones in a twitch. What to do about it was the problem.

Keeping her distance from him would be one answer, but that was impossible when she not only worked with the man on a daily basis but also lived next door to him.

So she'd have to fake it—pretend to a platonic neighbourliness she was far from feeling.

'The Frisky Fish is the best for fish and chips, or it was last time I bought any.' She finished dressing Hamish and straightened up as Angus, his body now suitably covered, came to join them.

'That one just across the road?'

Such a simple question but his accent really was to die for! She was thinking accents when she should have been answering but now it was too late, for he was speaking again.

'I'll buy our dinner,' he announced. 'I know what Hamish eats, what about you—a serve of fish and chips?'

The dark eyes were fixed on her face and Kate found it hard to pretend when just this casual regard made her feel warm inside.

'I'm more a calamari person—not into fish at all—and could I have a battered sav, as well?'

'Battered sav?' Again man and boy made a chorus of the question, though Hamish added, 'Oh, I want one of those, as well.'

'Just ask for it, you'll see,' Kate told Angus, smiling at his bewildered frown. 'Hamish and I will bag us a table.'

She took the excited little boy by the hand and they walked through the park until they found a vacant table.

'I'm going to kindy tomorrow—Dad's taking me,' Hamish told her, and though he sounded excited there was a hint of anxiety in his blue eyes.

'That will be such fun for you,' Kate said. 'Meeting lots of new friends, finding people to play with at the weekends. Maybe we can bring some of your friends to the beach one day.'

'When I can ride the waves so I can show them,'

Hamish told her, and Kate wondered at what age children developed a competitive streak.

She asked about his friends back in America and laughed at the adventures he and McTavish had shared, so she was surprised to see nearly an hour had passed and Angus hadn't returned. The Frisky Fish was popular and you usually had a wait while your meal was cooked, but this long?

'Here's Dad! He's remembered drinks even though we didn't tell him.'

Kate turned to see Angus approaching, holding white-wrapped parcels of food in one hand, a soft drink and a long green bottle in the other. He reached the table and put down the white parcels, gave Hamish his drink, then deposited the bottle on the table.

'I haven't a clue about Australian wines. I drank a fair bit of it in the U.S., but none of the names were familiar so I asked the chap behind the counter what went with battered savs.'

He was pulling two wineglasses from his pocket as he spoke, then he looked apologetically at Kate.

'I do hope you drink wine. I didn't think— should I have got you a soda, as well?'

'I'd love a glass of wine,' Kate assured him. 'Especially a glass of this wine. The bloke at the wine shop saw you coming, and sold you something really special—really expensive, I would think!'

Angus smiled at her, destroying most of her resolution to pretend she felt no attraction.

'Phooey to the price, as long as you enjoy it. We can both have a glass now and you can take the rest home to enjoy another time—it's a screw-top.'

He poured the wine, then busied himself unwrapping Hamish's dinner, showing him the battered sav.

'It's a kind of sausage called a saveloy that's fried in batter,' he explained to Hamish, who was squeezing tomato sauce onto it with the ease of an expert in takeaway food.

'And don't think you'll get one too often,' Angus added. 'Full of nitrates, then the batter and the frying in oil—just about every dietary and digestive no-no.'

'You're just jealous you didn't get one,' Kate told him, biting into hers with relish, then she laughed as Angus delved into his white package and came up with one.

'Well, I had to try it, didn't I?' he said defensively, but as he bit into it, he pulled a face and set it back down, deciding to eat his fish—grilled not fried, Kate noticed—instead.

'They're not to everyone's taste,' she said, 'but my father was the food police like you and I never got to taste one as a child, so I became obsessed later on in life.'

'Obsessed by battered savs?' Angus teased.

'Better than being obsessed by some other things I could think of,' Kate retorted.

Her next-door neighbour for one!

CHAPTER FOUR

KATE stopped the car in the back lane outside their gate and watched the two males walk into their yard, the taller one looking straight ahead, although Hamish was chattering at him.

He was a good father, Angus, Kate told herself as she pulled into the shed that did service as a garage for Molly, but she sensed that something was amiss in his relationship with his son. Back when she was young, she'd felt guilt—blamed herself—for her family's disintegration, thinking that if somehow she had managed to save Susie, everything would have been all right. It was this, she knew, that had led her to accept that, although her father loved her, there would always be a wall between them, so even when he was dying they couldn't talk about the past.

Had his wife's death built the same kind of wall

between Angus and Hamish, or had Angus simply shut himself off from *all* emotion to shield himself from further pain?

And just what did she think she was doing, pondering such things? she asked herself as she closed the double doors of the shed. Why was she considering the convoluted emotional state of someone she barely knew?

Because you're interested in him.

The answer was immediate and so obvious she felt a blush rising in her cheeks and was glad that Angus wasn't around to see it. A dead giveaway, her blushes.

She thought of Clare instead, of the dark-haired beauty, and reminded herself that if Angus McDowell decided to be interested in a woman on their team, then Clare would surely be the number-one choice.

Kate grumped her way inside, a depression she rarely felt dogging her footsteps, but as she showered she thought of baby Bob and realised how little she really had to complain about.

Refreshed, she opted not for lounging-at-home

clothes—in her case a singlet top and boxer shorts, her pyjamas of choice—but for respectable clothes—long shorts and a T-shirt, reasonable hospital visiting clothes. She'd just pop up and check not only on Bob but on Mr and Mrs Stamford, as well, to see how they were coping.

'There's something wrong? You've been called in?'

The panic she'd felt when she saw Angus by Bob's crib was evident in her voice, but when he turned and smiled at her she realised she'd overreacted.

'Did you think you were the only one who likes to check on patients, even when there's no reason for alarm?' he said.

Damn the blush.

'Of course not,' she managed stoutly. 'It was just that seeing you there with him gave me a shock. Mr and Mrs Stamford?'

'Gone to get a bite to eat. I said I'd stay.'

Was there an edge of strain in his voice that the statement pinged some memory in Kate's head?

'I got the impression you didn't like getting too involved with patients and their parents?'

He frowned at her but she was getting used to that.

'I think a certain degree of emotional detachment is necessary in our job.'

But even as Angus said the words he knew it hadn't always been that way. He also knew that it was seeing Kate Armstrong's empathy with Mrs Stamford that had broken through a little of his own detachment, enough to lead him to suggest he stayed with Bob while the couple ate together.

Was this good or bad, the breakthrough?

He was so caught up in his own thoughts it took him a moment to realise Kate was talking to him, pointing out the oxygen level in Bob's blood, suggesting they might be able to take him off the ventilator sooner, rather than later.

Dragging his mind back to his patient, he nodded his agreement.

'The operation is so much simpler when the coronary arteries are good,' he said. 'I was thinking the same thing about the ventilator when you came in. Maybe tomorrow morning we'll try him off it.'

They stood together beside the crib, Angus so conscious of the woman by his side he knew he had to be very, very wary of any contact with her outside working hours. Admittedly, her taking them to the beach, her offer to lend her car at the weekend, were nothing more than neighbourly gestures, and he wouldn't want to rebuff her or offend her, but every cell in his body was shouting a warning at him—danger, keep clear, problems ahead.

Kate felt him closing off from her and wondered if he'd been offended by her comment earlier—the one about detachment. But if he *was* closing off from her, well, that was good. It would be easier for her to pretend that's all they were, neighbourly colleagues, in spite of how her body felt whenever she was in his company.

She felt hot and excited and trembly somehow, physical manifestations she couldn't remember feeling since she was fifteen and had had a crush on the captain of the school's football team. Not that he'd ever looked at her, nor even stood close to her.

She stepped away from the crib, turning to greet the Stamfords, who'd returned from their dinner.

Pete Stamford eyed her with suspicion, and she wondered if he was worrying again, thinking the presence of two doctors by his son's crib meant there were problems.

'It's a habit,' Kate was quick to assure him. 'I find I sleep better if I do a final check of my patients before I go to bed.'

Pete nodded and Mrs Stamford, who still hadn't offered them the use of her first name, shook her head.

'Maybe all the horror stories we hear about health care are exaggerated,' she said, and Kate knew it was an apology for her anger of the morning.

'I don't think the news channels would attract an audience if they didn't exaggerate a bit,' she said, then she said goodnight to the couple, including Angus in the farewell, and left the PICU.

Angus caught up with her in the elevator foyer, and though he'd told himself he should linger with the Stamfords until Kate was well away from the hospital, he felt uncomfortable about her walking home on her own this late at night.

'Oh, I do it all the time,' she said when he mentioned the folly of a woman walking the streets on her own. 'There are always people around near the hospital. Cars and ambulances coming and going, police vehicles—we're not quite in the middle of the city, but we're close enough and the streets are well-lit.'

'There's that dark park across the road,' he told her, stepping into the elevator beside her and wondering if it was the enclosed space, or her presence within it, that was making him feel edgy.

'The park's well-lit, as well,' she told him, smiling up at him. 'I'm not totally stupid, you know. I wouldn't take any risks with my personal safety, but around here, well, you'll see.'

And see he did, for there *were* plenty of people around as they walked down the street towards their houses. People, cars, ambulances and, yes, police vehicles.

Too many people really.

Far too many!

The thought jolted him—hadn't he just decided that Kate was nothing more than a neighbourly colleague? But the light steps of the slim woman by his side, the upright carriage and slight tilt of her head when she turned towards him…something about her presence was physically disturbing. So much so he wanted to touch her, to feel her skin and the bones beneath it, to tilt her head just a little bit more, run his fingers into the tangled red hair and drop a kiss on lips so full and pink they drew him like a magnet.

Attraction, that's all it was. He could cope with it, ignore it. And tomorrow he had a full day of appointments, no operations, so he wouldn't see her. All he had to do was walk her home, say goodnight and that was that.

Except that Hamish was sitting in her front yard on the discarded yellow couch!

Admittedly Juanita was beside him, but still Angus felt the anger rise inside him.

'You should be in bed,' he told his son, his voice stern enough to make the child slide closer to his nanny.

'McTavish is sick,' Hamish whispered, and the woman Angus was ignoring reacted far more quickly than he did. She knelt in front of his child and took him in her arms.

'It's probably just the water here in Sydney,' she assured him. 'I get sick when I go to different cities and drink different water. But the sickness doesn't last. It's always over in a day or two.'

Was this why children needed a mother?

Because women reacted more instantly—instinctively perhaps—to a child's misery?

His mind had gone to McTavish's health, to wondering what could be wrong with the dog. And to the other puzzle Hamish's presence presented. He went with that because it was useless to speculate about the dog's illness.

'And just why does that mean you're sitting in

Dr Armstrong's yard, not at home in our living room?'

'Because Kate has a car and she *said* I could call her Kate!'

For a very biddable little boy there was a touch of defiance in the words and Angus found himself frowning, though at Juanita this time.

'What exactly is going on?' he demanded.

She shrugged her thick shoulders.

'It's as he says. The quarantine office phoned to say McTavish wasn't eating and there was nothing for it, but Hamish had to visit him, although I told him we couldn't see him tonight. He insisted he come and wait for his friend, sure she'd take him to see the dog.'

Angus could imagine what had happened, and understood that if Juanita had tried to insist on Hamish going to bed, the little boy would only have grown more upset, and with the move, and missing his dog, he was already emotionally out of balance.

But knowing how this had come about didn't help him in deciding what to do, although now

Kate Armstrong seemed to have taken things into her own hands. She was sitting on the couch beside Juanita, holding Hamish on her lap.

'Juanita's right,' she was telling Hamish, 'we can't visit McTavish at this time of night because if we did all the other dogs and cats and birds and horses there would be disturbed and upset and they would want their owners to be visiting them, as well. But your father can phone them and ask them how McTavish is now. Perhaps he can tell them what McTavish's favourite food is, and the people who are minding him can try to coax him to eat a little of it. They have vets—animal doctors—at the quarantine centre who will be looking after him, just as your Dad looks after the babies at the hospital.'

'My mother died.'

Angus's heart stopped beating for an instant and a chill ran through his body. He'd never heard Hamish mention his mother, but it was obvious the little boy assumed Jenna had been ill before she died, and now he was thinking McTavish could also die. He knelt in front of his son and lifted him from Kate's knee.

'McTavish won't die,' he promised, knowing the assurance was needed, although he also knew he couldn't guarantee such a thing. 'Kate's right, let's go inside and phone the quarantine centre and tell them that he really likes—'

What did the dog really like?

'Biscuits,' Hamish told him, his fears forgotten in this new excitement.

'Not exactly a dietary imperative,' Angus muttered, but if biscuits could coax McTavish to eat, then he'd certainly suggest them.

He carried his son towards the house, pausing for Juanita to catch up with them and to nod goodnight to Kate. But the image of her sitting on the old yellow couch, his son in her arms, remained with him long after his conversation with the quarantine office and the reassuring return phone call that, yes, McTavish had eaten some biscuits and even eaten some of the dried dog food the carers had mixed in with the broken biscuits.

The image of her accompanied him to bed,

aware of her in the house next door, so close, too close.

Any woman would have comforted Hamish in that situation, he told himself, but some instinct deep inside was telling him she wasn't just any woman, this Kate Armstrong. She was special—special in a way no woman had been since Jenna.

Which was another reason he had to avoid her....

It proved, as he'd known it would, impossible, for the teams met regularly. He operated with her, and discussion of patients was inevitable. But he managed to avoid her out of work hours until the day he came home early enough to attack the hedge around the garden gate.

Kate had been sensible in suggesting that if Hamish wanted to adventure he do it in her backyard, so freeing the gate had become a necessity. He'd bought a pair of hedge trimmers at the local hardware store and, some three-quarters of an hour of reasonably hard labour later, had cleared his side enough to push the gate open. Now all he had to do was trim her side.

Should he phone her first to ask if it was okay to come in and do it?

Phone her when she lived next door?

Well, he wasn't going to go over and ask; just seeing her each day at work was enough to tell him the attraction was going to take a long time to die.

He was debating this when Hamish returned from his job of stacking all the cut-off hedge branches in a pile near the back fence.

'Oh, look, we can get into Kate's garden.'

He ran through the gate before Angus could stop him, calling back to his father in even greater excitement, 'And here's Kate, she's right up a ladder!'

Right up a ladder?

A child suddenly calling out?

She could be startled!

Fall!

Angus dashed through the open gate to find his son confidently climbing up a very long ladder, at the top of which stood the team anaesthetist, a measuring tape, a pen and a notebook clamped in her hand.

She was peering down uncertainly, no doubt partly because Hamish's enthusiastic attack on the ladder rungs was making it wobble.

'No, Hamish dear,' she said gently. 'You can't have two people on a ladder at once. It might tip over.'

Once again the first thought, beyond the anger fear had wrought in his chest, was that this woman would make a wonderful mother. She was always fair. She always explained in a common-sense way that a child would understand.

Although, Angus realised a little belatedly, the child in question hadn't taken much notice and was still six rungs up the ladder and teetering there a little uncertainly.

Angus rescued him, set him on the ground, then looked up at the woman above him.

'And just what are you doing up there?'

He'd meant it as a neighbourly question, but it came out as a demand because the ladder seemed old and highly unstable and she was at the roof level of a two-storey house.

'Possums,' she replied, apparently not taking exception to his tone. 'I wouldn't mind the little beggars living in the roof if they'd just stay in one place, but it seems they live on one side and feed on the other so they're galloping across my ceiling in what sound like hobnail boots all night.'

'Possums?'

He realised there'd been a lot of conversation after that, but his mind had stuck on the word.

'Little furry animals, big eyes and long tails, cute as all get out but *not* much fun if they're living in your ceiling.'

'Oh!'

The word was obviously inadequate but Angus wasn't certain where to take the conversation next, and the uncertainty was only partly to do with the fact that Kate appeared to be wearing very short shorts, so from where he stood her pale legs went on forever and he found it hard to focus on anything else.

Fortunately Hamish was less inhibited.

'Possums!' he shrieked. 'Can I see them? Can I, Kate, can I?'

'Later,' she said. 'Just let me finish here and I'll come down and explain.'

Angus found himself wanting to order her down right away—wanting to tell her he'd do whatever it was she was doing—but having no notion of possums' habits, nor of what she could be arranging for them, he knew he'd be making a fool of himself if he said anything at all. So he stood and held the ladder steady, and not, he told himself, so he could watch her as she climbed down it. In fact, he turned resolutely away, determined not to have his resolve weakened by long pale legs in short shorts.

Kate told herself that of course she could climb down a ladder that Angus was holding; after all, hadn't she been successful in avoiding him these past few days, limiting their encounters to purely work contact? But her legs trembled as she came closer to where he stood and it took an effort of supreme will not to climb back up the ladder and perch on the roof until he grew tired of standing there.

'What exactly were you doing?' he asked as she passed him, very close—close enough to see a beard shadow on his cheeks and lines of tiredness around his eyes.

Wasn't he sleeping well?

She wasn't exactly enjoying night-times herself, finding it hard to sleep when images of him kept flitting through her mind.

He was so *close*....

'There's a hole,' she said, reaching the ground and backing away from him, lifting a hand to stop him moving the ladder. 'That's how they're getting in and out. I had to measure it.'

'So you could make a door for them?' Hamish asked, dancing around with excitement at the thought of a possum door.

'Not exactly,' Kate admitted, 'although I suppose you could call it a door, but I intend to keep it locked.'

'You want to lock them in?' Angus asked. It must be something to do with the air in Australia that so many of the conversations he had with Kate had a feeling of unreality about them. Battered savs came to mind....

'So I can keep them out,' she replied, speaking to him but squatting down so her face was level with Hamish's. 'There are plenty of other places the possums can live, think of all the trees here and in the park. That's where possums should live—in holes in the trunks and thick branches of trees. Once I fix my hole, they'll find somewhere else very easily.'

Hamish nodded his understanding, then asked the obvious question.

'But how will you get them out?'

Kate smiled at him, though Angus imagined there was sadness in the smile. Was she hurting for her own lack of children? Were they *so* very important to her?

Maybe one child would do her?

Hamish—

The thought shocked him so much he straightened his spine and clamped down on his wandering mind, thinking he'd go and cut the hedge on this side, departing forthwith, but she was talking again, explaining to Hamish, and Angus couldn't help but listen.

'I've been feeding them every night since I came back here to live,' she told Hamish. 'Are you allowed to stay up until eight o'clock because that's when it starts to get dark and they come out of the roof and down here to the garden to eat the fruit I put out. There's a whole possum family—a mother and a father and two little ones that sometimes ride on their mother's back but who are learning to climb themselves now.'

'Can I come and see, can I, Dad?'

The excitement in his son's voice meant Angus had to look at him, *really* look at him, something he usually avoided as Hamish's resemblance to Jenna was like a knife blade going through his skin.

And the excitement in Hamish's voice was mirrored in his little face. Seeing it, Angus could only nod. He even found himself smiling.

'You'll come and see them, too?' Hamish persisted, and Angus lost his smile, knowing for sure he'd have suggested Juanita take the little boy to see the possums. It wasn't that he didn't love Hamish dearly, but with the move and settling in to a new routine, the bond between himself and Hamish had seemed to weaken rather than strengthen. Besides which, more out-of-work hours' proximity to Kate Armstrong was something he needed to avoid.

'Of course,' he responded, suddenly aware that it was selfish to refuse—a kind of self-protection because Hamish looked so like Jenna.

Angus didn't sound overly excited by the idea, Kate decided, but then she wasn't so chuffed, either. She wanted to see less of Angus McDowell, not more.

'Eight o'clock, then,' she said, and headed for the shed where she hoped she'd find a piece of timber the size she wanted. Unfortunately the gate was in that direction so Angus fell in beside her, while Hamish raced excitedly back to his place to tell Juanita about the possums.

'Just what do you intend doing about the hole?' Angus asked.

Ah, easy question!

'I'll cut a piece of timber to fit over it and nail it in place. From the look of it, someone's tried to fix it before using some kind of magic glue to stick fibro over the hole but the possums were too cunning for that. They just ate the glue, or got rid of it some other way.'

She realised Angus had stopped walking and turned back to check on him. He was standing stock-still, staring at her with an unreadable expression on his face.

'What's up?' she asked, although she knew what was wrong with *her*. Just looking at the man raised her heart rate.

'The way I figure it, you wait until the possums come out, then you go and cover their hole, that right?'

Kate nodded.

'Up that rickety old ladder, *and* in the dark because they won't come out 'til dusk? You were going to do that yourself, telling no-one who'd go looking for you if you fell, asking no-one for help?'

Kate nodded again, although she was starting to feel peeved. It was none of his damn business what she did, yet he was sounding like a father admonishing a wayward teen.

'Didn't it occur to you how dangerous that was?' he demanded, and she forgot peeved and smiled.

'Angus,' she said gently, 'this is the twenty-first century. Women do these things. They take care of themselves, and if that includes minor repairs to their homes, then that's part of it. Actually,' she added after a momentary pause, 'they've been doing it for centuries. I bet it was often the woman who climbed on top of the cave to move dirt and stones over places where the rain got in. The men would have been off chasing bears and wouldn't have considered a bit of water over the fire an inconvenience.'

'I wasn't thinking about sexism or what women can or can't do. There's a safety issue,' he countered, but something in the way he said it didn't ring true.

Kate, however, went along with him.

'The ladder might look rickety but it's perfectly safe,' she assured him, but he didn't look any happier than he had when the whole stupid conversation had begun.

They parted, Kate leaving Angus hacking at the hedge while she continued on to the shed, not thinking about oddments of timber at all, but about a little warm place inside her that seemed to think Angus's concern might have been personal.

Fortunately it turned out to be one of those afternoons when the sensible part of her brain held sway. It seemed to laugh so loudly at the thoughts of the emotional part that she knew she'd got it wrong.

Which was just as well, she told herself, although a heaviness in her chest told her she did not believe that at all!

CHAPTER FIVE

THEY came, the tall man and the child, as dusk was falling, filling Kate's backyard with shadows. Urging Hamish to talk softly, she led them into her kitchen and lifted him onto the bench beneath the window.

'See,' she said quietly, 'just there under the lemon tree, I've a little table with cut-up apple and banana and some cherries on it.'

She had the outside light on, knowing its soft yellow glow didn't disturb the nocturnal animals.

Holding Hamish steady on the bench, she was aware of Angus moving up behind her, aware of the warmth of his body close, and even the scent of him, citrusy yet still male. It was some primordial instinct that had her body responding, she told herself, trying hard to concentrate on Hamish in order to blot out the effect Angus was having on her hormones.

'Listen,' she whispered to Hamish, 'can you hear them scrabbling down the tree?'

Hamish nodded, his little body rigid in her hands, though she could feel excitement thrumming through him. The longing for a child—her child, family—zapped through her like an electric current, shocking her with its intensity. It had to be because she was holding Hamish, because normally the longing was no more than a vaguely felt dull ache.

Well, at least it had shocked her out of focusing on the man behind her.

'Look, Dad, look!' Hamish said excitedly, and Kate was happy to yield her place to Angus so he could hold his son and share the excitement as the small furry animals with their pointed noses and big bright brown eyes landed on the fruit table, the older pair looking around, checking their safety, while the two youngsters began to eat.

'Oh, they've got little hands!' Hamish cried as one of the possums turned towards them, a piece of apple in its paws, sharp white teeth nibbling at it.

'They've got wonderfully expressive faces,' Angus said, a note of genuine delight in his voice as he turned to smile at Kate.

'I know,' she agreed, 'and I love them to bits, but they are *not* going to continue living in my ceiling!'

They watched in silence, broken only now and then by Hamish's exclamations of wonder and delight. Then, the feast finished, the possums leapt into the branches of the lemon tree and, from there, scrambled into a jacaranda, scurrying up the trunk, then out along one of the top branches, from which they leapt into a eucalypt.

'There's a hole in the trunk of that tree where they can live,' Kate told Hamish. 'They could go and live in the park but they probably won't because they know they get fresh fruit here every night.'

She'd lifted him off the bench and carried him outside as the possums departed, and though she enjoyed the heaviness of his tired body in her

arms she knew she had to hand him over to his
father.

'Can I come and see them again?'

She was about to answer when she realised it
was probably way past his bedtime. Fortunately
Angus answered for her.

'Perhaps in winter when it gets dark earlier,' he
said, 'although maybe we should think about putting out some fruit some nights, just as we used
to put out bird feed for the birds in winter back
home.'

Back home!

The phrase echoed in Kate's head as Angus
lifted his son from her arms and, after thanking
her, walked towards the gate in the hedge.

It was a reminder that on top of all the other
reasons she shouldn't be attracted to this man, he
didn't really belong here. Although as far as she
knew he wasn't on a time-limited contract. Silly
woman! Stop thinking about him. Get on with
the job you have to do!

Angus kissed Hamish goodnight and left him
with Juanita, determined to get back to Kate's

place before she began her precarious task on the ladder. He'd go up and do it himself, and to hell with her 'liberated woman' attitude. After all, what use was an injured anaesthetist to him?

Too late! By the time he returned to his back-yard she was already at the top of the ladder, and he could hear the hammering even before he walked through the gate.

Now he was in a dilemma! He didn't want to startle her, but he couldn't *not* approach. The least he could do was hold the ladder steady.

'I've come back,' he said, speaking quietly. 'And if you climb down, I'll do that for you.'

'I'm nearly done,' she answered cheerfully. 'Once I had the size it really wasn't difficult. There were studs under the soffit I could nail to, and though I feel just the teensiest bit guilty about shutting the family out of their home, at least I'll get to sleep more easily.'

'Which is more than I'm doing at the moment,' Angus muttered to himself.

He only realised he'd spoken the thought out loud when Kate said, 'I beg your pardon?'

'Oh, nothing,' he told her. 'I was just wondering why you haven't someone in your life you can get to do these jobs.'

Well, he *had* been wondering that earlier! The 'someone' might be a boyfriend or partner and he was far more curious about her single status than he should be!

'Are we back on the "man's job" thing?' she asked, beginning to come down the ladder so it moved in his hands.

'Not really,' he admitted, 'but it's hard for most men to think a woman is just as capable at odd jobs as they are. In fact, you're probably far more capable than I am. I'm a total fool when it comes to hammers—I seem to hit everything but the nail.'

Blithering, that's what his mother would say he was doing, but as Kate came closer he realised he'd either have to change the way he was holding the ladder, or let her finish her climb to the ground right through his arms.

The silly conversation ceased but he couldn't let go of the ladder, and although he pushed himself as far back as he could he still feel her body slither against his as she reached the lower rungs. A slight sway of the ladder and she was in his arms, all reason forgotten as he lifted her off the second bottom rung, setting her on the ground, turning her, kissing her, kissing her with the desperation of a—

He had no idea how to classify his desperation— just knew it existed, for his hands were clamped around her body and his lips were pressed to hers, his tongue already exploring the taste of her, the shape of her lips, the hardness of those neat white teeth....

It could have been a minute or an hour later that she moved against him, pulling back, smiling weakly at him in the yellow outdoor light.

'Surely only a fool would kiss a woman with a hammer in her hand,' she said, but though her voice was steady, he could see the unevenness in her breathing, see the way she was drawing air deep into her lungs. To replenish what she'd lost during the kiss or to steady her heartbeats as he was trying to steady his?

She should have hit him with the hammer, Kate thought as she waved the tool aloft. Or hit herself! Her heart thudded in her chest and no amount of denial or sensible talk could convince her she *wasn't* attracted to this man.

'I don't do serious relationships.' The words were as blunt as hammer hits would be, his voice deep and husky as if he'd had to force it out past innumerable obstacles.

Keep it light! Kate warned herself.

'And you're telling me this, why?'

She even managed a smile as she asked.

'Because I'm about to kiss you again and I thought you should know,' he said, and before she had time to make sense of the statement, he'd turned the words to action. He reached out, removed the hammer from her hand and dropped it on the ground. One arm clamped around her, drawing her close against his body, tucking her into it as if to fit a missing piece of a jigsaw puzzle, then the fingers of his free hand grazed her chin, tipping her head, fingers running into her hair.

By the time his lips met hers, Kate was breathless

with the delay, her body throbbing with a desire she'd never felt before. Had he felt it, tasted it with the brush of lips on lips, so that his mouth became demanding, insistent, forcing her lips open as if he needed to claim all he could of her in a kiss?

She was melting, floating, boneless in his arms, held upright by his strong hand against her back, the other tangled in her hair. And he murmured as he kissed—muttered, really—little words and sounds she really couldn't make out, although they sounded more like reprimands than endearments.

But the noise did nothing to diminish the potency of the kiss. If anything, it intensified the excitement, so when Kate realised she was making little moaning noises, she didn't try to stop them. She surrendered to sensation, enjoying the searing heat of desire along her nerves, the burning need settling at the base of her abdomen.

Crazy as a loon! Angus didn't think he'd ever used the expression he'd heard often in the U.S., but it was the only one that seemed to fit. Yet even as it echoed in his head, and he chided himself for his behaviour, he couldn't take his lips from hers, couldn't release her body from his clasp. He wanted her—dear heaven but he wanted her—and kissing her like this, feeling her response, there was only one place they'd end up and that was in bed.

Hers, obviously. He'd never paraded any of the women he'd occasionally enjoyed relationships with in front of Hamish.

She was so slight and delicate, like quicksilver in his arms, yet the breasts he could feel against his chest were real and soft and full and, as his hand slid to her butt, he felt its curves. But it was her mouth that still demanded most of his attention. Syrup sweet, that mouth! Maple syrup! Years in the States had given him a taste for it and now he tasted it in Kate—addictive.

Then she was gone, warm night air where her body had been, a distance of perhaps a foot between them.

'*Not* a good idea, Dr McDowell,' she said, although the flush on her cheeks and the glitter in her eyes suggested otherwise.

'You're going to deny there's an attraction between us?' He was still trying to work out how she'd slipped away from him, while thwarted lust was making him tetchy.

'Of course not.' She shook her head to emphasise the words, the wild red curls flying every which way. 'It'd be easier to deny the sun rising, but that's all it is, Angus, attraction, and at my age I really don't want a go-nowhere affair. If I'm putting time and energy into a relationship, then I'd like to think there might be some future in it.'

'So every relationship should lead to marriage? Is that what you're saying?' Maybe he was a tad more than tetchy!

'Of course not,' she snapped. 'I'm not entirely stupid. But I don't see the point of going into a relationship that has nowhere to go and you've made it clear anything between us *would* have nowhere to go. What was it you said? "I don't do serious relationships"? Well, that's fine, and I like the fact you set out the guidelines from the beginning, but I'm entitled to do the same, and I don't want to go into something just for the sex.'

'It wouldn't just be sex,' Angus muttered— not good that he was down to muttering already. Muttering was usually part of losing an argument. But he persevered anyway. 'We enjoy each other's company. We can have dinner, go to the theatre—'

Kate couldn't help but laugh, shaking her head at her behaviour at the same time, but unable to control the gurgles of mirth that were bubbling up from deep within her.

'Oh, Angus, if you could only hear yourself. We could go to dinner—yep, and then back to my place to bed. We could go to the theatre and—'

'Okay, I get your point,' he growled. 'I can even see it from your side and understand, but don't think for a moment this discussion is over because whatever it is between us is so strong I doubt either of us can resist it.'

The growl became a husky whisper as he added, 'Or can you?' before he took her in his arms and his mouth claimed hers once again.

Enjoy it while you can. That was Kate's last rational thought before sensation took over and she floated on the blissful cloud of desire he seemed to generate so easily.

It couldn't just be the way he kissed.

The thought eased into her head as she turned her lips away from his to catch her breath. There had to be more to the way he made her feel than just kissing. Perhaps the way her body fitted his had something to do with it. She pressed experimentally closer and went back to kissing. But not mindlessly this time, for her sensible brain was chiding her the whole time

Idiocy! Plain and simple. Stop before it becomes impossible to stop.

But she couldn't—wouldn't—because kissing Angus was the most exciting, enthralling, stupendous thing she'd ever done...well, that she could think of right now! Perhaps if they kept to kissing, a kissing relationship...

'You're not behaving like someone who doesn't want to get involved with me.'

The accusation was delivered with a warm

breath close to her left ear and she shivered as his tongue flicked, then his teeth nibbled gently on her earlobe.

'I never denied the attraction,' she whispered back, kissing him this time, pressing her lips to his as a punctuation mark at the end of the sentence. Then a sigh filtered out and she pushed away.

'I do mean it, Angus. I really don't want to go into a pointless relationship—'

He moved but not so far away that he couldn't still clasp her loosely, holding her within the circle of his arms so his strong features were in profile against the yellow light and she could see his lips—*those* lips—move as he spoke.

'A lot of relationships turn out to be pointless,' he reminded her. 'There are never guarantees that everything will work out. Surely it's not so much how you go into them as how you come out of them.'

A hopeless mess, that's how I'd come out of a relationship with you, Kate thought, but she didn't say it. I've done that before and really do not want to do it again.

He was making some kind of point here, and she should have an argument to counter it, but her brain was still fuddled from the kissing and her body was suddenly very, very tired.

'I am not going to argue semantics with you tonight,' she said, then regretted saying anything when he grinned at her and restarted all the fizzing sensations that had been happening along her nerves.

'Aha, so that means we'll have another night to argue them.'

He was teasing her and suddenly she hated him—well, not hated, but definitely didn't like him very much. He'd awoken responses from her she'd never thought to feel and to him it was nothing more than a game—kissing, flirtation, an affair—with no more point than the kissing games young teens played at parties, practicing for love....

'Go home,' she told him, and though his arms

tightened momentarily around her, she stiffened and he didn't pull her close.

'No goodnight kiss?'

'No kisses period,' she told him, but as he walked towards the gate she remembered it was Friday night and called him back. 'Wait, I'll give you the car keys and the sat nav so you can take the car to visit McTavish. I might not be here in the morning.'

Angus turned and followed her into the house, into the kitchen, the only room he'd seen so far. She rummaged through a drawer in search of keys while he studied her, wondering why this woman of all the women he met in his day-to-day life should fire something in him, something so strong he knew he should be strengthening his resistance against her, not wondering how soon he could kiss her again.

'Ah,' she said, turning to him with triumph in her eyes, her smile so open and delighted he felt as if a hand had tightened around his heart. 'Not only keys but the sat nav, as well. You've used one? Can program it?'

He took the little device and nodded, knowing it was the same brand as the one he'd used in the U.S., but the hand clutching his heart hadn't let go and he suspected he'd have to rethink his ambition to kiss Kate again as soon as possible. He was beginning to suspect that kissing Kate could be addictive, and addictions were hard to break....

'Thank you,' he said, aware he sounded formal and aloof once more, the way he sounded at the hospital when he was talking to the parents of his patients.

And Kate heard it, too, for her dark eyebrows rose and her pink lips, still swollen from his kisses, twisted into a wry smile.

'Okay,' she said, as if she understood exactly what his tone had meant. 'Enjoy yourselves tomorrow. There's plenty of fuel in the tank if you want to take Hamish to the beach after you've been to the quarantine station.'

He nodded and departed, pausing in the doorway to look back at her, the smile gone from her face and in its place an unmistakeable sadness.

'Goodnight,' he said, for what else was there to

say. An affair between them could *not* have any point and he wasn't going to lie to her to get her into bed.

Although, as he shut the gate between their properties, the discomfort in his body suggested that this stance was all very well morally and ethically, but physically, given that he wouldn't be able to avoid seeing her every working day, it might be difficult.

Kate was actually pleased when the phone rang at one o'clock in the morning. She might have been in a light sleep but whatever sleep she'd managed had been deeply disturbed, her body tossing and turning, feeling the magic Angus had generated, the heat, and wanting to satisfy it.

It was a good thing she was mentally strong, she told herself as she pulled on slacks and a T-shirt. She had a stock of laundered white coats in her locker at work, so all she had to do was clean her teeth, wash her face, tie her hair up in a bundle and get moving up the road.

A five-day-old baby girl had been admitted to

the hospital with cold, clammy skin, rapid breathing and alarming cyanosis, her lips very blue. The neonatologist on call was doing X-rays, an ECG and an echocardiogram, but had called in one of Kate's team—she rather thought Oliver was on call this weekend—thinking they'd need to do a cardiac catheterisation to see what was happening in the baby's heart.

Kate considered what lay ahead as she jogged up the street, thinking, too, of the parents, so happy with their new baby, then panicked by her distress. She made her way to the treatment room off the PICU where she found not Oliver but Angus.

'You're not on call,' she told him, so bothered by the unexpected encounter her heart was racing and her mind in a whirl—not a good way to be before sedating a tiny baby.

'Oliver had a family occasion of some kind so I offered to do tonight for him. He'll owe me.'

Well! Obviously Angus was in hospital mode, all thoughts of hot kisses in her backyard well and truly gone.

Which is how it should be, she reminded herself.

And if he could do it, so could she!

'How long will you need?' she asked as she read the baby's chart, checking her weight so the sedation could be accurately measured.

Angus didn't answer immediately, but she was used to that now. She could imagine him running through the operation in his mind—inserting the catheter into a blood vessel in the patient's groin, feeding the wire carefully up into the heart, perhaps introducing dye so he could better see the problem, perhaps also, depending on what he found, needing to use a special catheter with a balloon at the tip to open up a hole between the left and right atria.

'Forty minutes! I should be able to do it in half an hour but we'll take the extra ten minutes just in case. It's a suspected TAPVR.'

Kate mentally translated the initials, thinking how frightening it must be for parents to hear that their child had total anomalous pulmonary venous return, when, in fact, it simply meant that the veins from the lungs, pulmonary veins, had somehow got themselves attached to the wrong part of the heart. Angus would find out exactly what was happening now, and later the baby would need an operation where the veins would be disconnected from where they were, and set into place where they should be, connecting to the left atrium. At the same time, the surgeon would close the little hole Angus was about to make, and the baby's heart should operate beautifully.

She checked the dosage of sedative and injected it into the intravenous line already attached to the baby girl, who lay, unresisting and lethargic, looking up at her until slowly the dark blue eyes closed and her breathing grew less laboured.

Kate took a blood sample from a second catheter in the baby's foot, wanting to check on the blood gases before the procedure, so they could compare it after Angus had completed the operation. A small oxygen monitor was attached to one of the tiny fingers, but Kate always checked the blood, as well, not wanting to rely on just one reading.

Angus nodded at her as if he agreed, then his eyes focused on the ultrasound screen as he slid the fine wire up the baby's vein towards the heart.

Kate watched her patient and the second monitor that told her exactly what was happening in the baby's body—blood pressure, oxygen saturation, heart rate and rhythm. She watched over the unconscious child while just a small part of her mind went back to the conversation she'd had with the nurse at baby Bob's monitor, the nurse who wanted to get out of the PICU before she had children because seeing the ones who had health issues made her nervous about having children of her own.

Yet Kate saw babies with congenital problems every day of her working life, so why didn't it bother her?

Because she knew they could be fixed?

Nonsense, not all of them could, although every day brought new procedures and treatments to improve the health not only of babies but of adults, as well.

But deep down she knew it didn't bother her because the longing for a child—or for the child she hadn't had—was far stronger than any fear of a congenital abnormality. It was gut deep, instinctually emotional—inexplicable really.…

The straying thoughts made her glance at Angus, his lips—those lips—closed into a thin line as he concentrated on getting the tip of the balloon catheter through a tiny opening in the atrial wall. As she had suggested to him once before, maybe it was his work with children that made him so definite about not having any more.

She'd have liked to ask him again, liked to have had him as a friend, as well as a neighbour and a colleague, but after the kisses, that was impossible.

'Impossible!' she repeated, actually saying the word, although under her breath, so she could drum it into her head.

Angus glanced her way before returning his attention to the monitor, where she saw him pull the tiny, now-inflated balloon through the hole, enlarging it so the oxygenated blood could mix with the unoxygenated blood and ease the work the little heart had to do while they waited for the baby to grow strong enough to have an operation.

'Impossible? No such word!' he told her, and she heard the satisfaction in his voice as he withdrew the catheter and dressed the wound in the baby's groin.

'You really love your job, don't you?' Kate said, and he gave her a quizzical look.

'Are you telling me you don't?'

She shrugged. Of course she loved her job, but it was far less demanding than a surgeon's, so the risk of burnout—of falling out of love with it—was far less likely.

'I doubt anyone could work with babies like this if they didn't love it,' the nurse who'd been assisting said. 'And as for Kate, well, I've seen her here at four in the morning, anxious about a patient she might have sedated days earlier, just drawn by some instinct to come back.'

Kate shook her head, although she did remember the incident—a baby newly off the ventilator having a reaction to some drug the surgeon had prescribed. To this day she couldn't say what had brought her racing to the hospital.

'I think they send out thought waves, our babies,' she said, smiling at the nurse. 'It wasn't only me that night—I found Phil here, as well. He'd woken up with a conviction that something was wrong so we were able to stabilise the baby and get him back onto a ventilator. He came off two days later without the slightest trouble.'

Angus nodded; he knew what she was saying, although he'd never realised other people had that inexplicable sense of trouble from time to time. He followed Kate from the treatment room, the nurse wheeling the baby back into the PICU. Kate stopped by Bob's crib, smiling down at Mrs Stamford, who slept beside her baby boy.

'He looks good,' she said quietly to Angus, and taking in the pink cheeks of the infant, Angus had to agree. But Kate looked good, as well, although why he found her so attractive he couldn't have explained. To another man she might just be a slim, average-looking woman with wild red hair, but just being in her vicinity stirred his senses in ways he didn't want to consider.

'I'll walk you home,' he said, but she shook her head.

'I'll stay awhile,' she said. 'You'd best be off. You have a big day ahead of you, navigating around Sydney for the first time, visiting McTavish.'

Angus would have liked to argue, but she was right. He hadn't been sleeping when the call came, still disturbed by the after-effects of kissing Kate. But now he could walk away from her—in colleague mode again.

No worries!

He said goodnight and went along the corridor to the elevator foyer, but the sense of her came with him—'kissing Kate,' not 'colleague Kate…'

CHAPTER SIX

KNOWING she could have other emergency calls so needed some sleep, Kate left the hospital an hour later, walking slowly past the house where Angus would be sleeping, trying hard to think about work, not her colleague. But the kisses had stirred something deep inside her, and she had to wonder if a relationship—forget that, an affair—with Angus would be so very bad.

Okay, so it had no future, but what else was she doing? Going through the motions of a life, her social life consisting of occasional visits to a movie, or having dinner at friends' places, where a likely man would have been invited, her friends all committed to 'finding a man for Kate'!

From time to time, one of these available men would follow up on their meeting, inviting her for drinks, maybe dinner, but after a few outings, too casual to be called dates, one or other of them would realise that there was no...zing—that was the only word—between them and the relationship would be over before it had really begun. Yet she'd always remained confident that somewhere out there was a man for her—*the* man—the one who'd be a father to her children, a grandfather to her grandchildren.

Or was she wasting her life? Letting it slip away from her because of the loss of an unborn baby years ago and an absurd dream she'd had as a child?

She'd found the zing—boy, had she found the zing!—and she was going to let it go because an affair with Angus had no future?

Was she out of her tiny mind?

She realised her steps had slowed sufficiently for it to be called a halt and she was standing on the footpath outside Angus's house, staring at it like some lovelorn fool.

She had to get her act together, sort out some priorities here. But even as she moved on, this idea firmly fixed in her mind, she imagined the weight of a tiny baby in her arms, and longed to feel it for herself—her own baby in her arms, the future in its tiny form....

She'd lied to Angus—perhaps not lied but shifted the emphasis of her dreams—when she'd talked of her ambition to be a grandmother. Yes, that had been the precipitating event, that long-ago family gathering, but later, after the miscarriage, it was a family of her own she longed for, a baby of her own, someone who belonged to her, had her blood, her genes—although probably not her red hair.

Of course, *belonged* was the wrong word—no one could belong to another person....

She unlocked her front door and walked into the house, hearing the ghosts of children who'd lived there in the past when it was the family home it was built to be. The smell of the chemical in the product she was using to strip wallpaper off the living room walls struck her immediately. Well, at least this weekend she'd have enough work to do finishing that job to keep her mind off Angus and relationships and babies of her own.

* * *

'We saw McTavish and he remembered me!'

Had she been kidding herself when she'd thought she'd see no more of the McDowells over the weekend? Had she forgotten that Hamish now viewed her as his new best friend? She was bundling the last strips of the wallpaper, slimy and stinking, into the rubbish bin near the back lane when he erupted from the tunnel in the hedge.

'I'm sure he remembered you,' Kate told the little boy, who was now holding his nose as he stared at her.

'Phew, you smell,' he told her, and she had to laugh. If anyone told it how it was, it was Hamish.

'I do indeed, but I'm about to have a shower. I've been peeling the old wallpaper off a wall and it's a very smelly job.'

'Can I look, can I?' he demanded, excited as he always seemed to be by some new concept.

'Only if you tell your father or Juanita first. Did you tell them you were coming over?'

'We were both coming over,' a deeper voice said

as Angus appeared through the gate. 'Hamish just took the shortcut.'

This time it wasn't just a cheek blush! Kate could feel her entire body heating, reddening, as she imagined just how she must look—scraps of wallpaper and stripping chemicals in her hair, bits sticking to her arms and legs. Her working attire, an ancient pair of cut-off jeans—cut off far too short—and an old T-shirt advertising a rock band long defunct.

'You found the place all right, then?'

It was a feeble response but she saw that Angus had her car keys and sat nav in his hand, and it was all she could manage.

'No problems,' he replied, although, possibly for the first time since she'd met him, she could see a gleam of what could only be humour in his dark eyes.

'Kate's pulled all the wallpaper off her walls and I'm going to look,' Hamish announced, breaking what could easily have become a strained silence, because her conversational spring had definitely dried up and he seemed content to stand there and study her dishevelled state—with that gleam in his eyes—for ever.

'We might be interrupting Kate,' Angus argued, but Hamish waved aside the objection.

'No, she was just going to have a shower, but we don't mind if she smells a bit, do we?'

Angus had to smile. Better to be smiling at his son's faux pas than be thinking of Kate stripped down in a shower. Why was stripping such a recurring theme in her backyard?

'Kate?' he said, and as he watched he saw her weigh her discomfort at having him in her house—and probably the smell—against the appeal in a pair of blue eyes. He saw her waver, then nod at Hamish.

"Okay,' she said, reluctance dragging out the word, 'you can come in but I warn you, there's nothing very exciting about a living room with bare damp walls. I thought I'd paint it once I had the wallpaper off, but it's kind of rough so maybe I'll have to repaper.'

She was leading the way into her house as she spoke, through the kitchen, up a hall, past a dining room and into the large room at the front of the house. Angus peered around, realising this house must have been similar to the one he was renting, before his place was converted into flats.

Hamish had climbed onto the window seat in one of two bay windows in the graciously designed room.

'If that hedge wasn't there, I could see my bedroom,' he said, excitedly working out the geography of the two places.

'In my house, I use that room as my study,' Kate told him. 'Do you want to see it?'

Hamish was off the window seat in a second, heading out of the room and across the hall. Angus followed more slowly, wondering at the very definite reluctance he was feeling. Was it something to do with seeing more of Kate's house and the possibility it might make him feel closer to her?

Or was it seeing how Hamish had connected with her that made him uneasy. She treated his son as she would an adult friend, accepting his enthusiasm for anything new and never speaking down to him. Once again Angus was conscious of a gap in his relationship with Hamish, and found himself frowning over the thought. He did things with his son—read him stories, listened to his prattle about his daily life—loved him dearly, but...

He turned his thoughts back to Kate but there was no less confusion there. The moment he saw the room he knew he'd have been better off not following, for this was obviously the room she'd chosen to furnish first, and though he didn't know her well, he knew the room spoke volumes about her. Two walls lined with bookshelves and books from childhood days with faded covers, through medical tomes and reference books to the latest thrillers, were crammed into the shelves. She had a desk, an old roll-top set against the third wall, but her laptop was on the cushioned window seat of yet another bay window and he could picture her there, checking something out, keeping up with friends through emails, perhaps doing something on the research she'd mentioned once.

The cushions on the window seat looked soft

and comfortable, blue and green tones, muted but easy colours with which to live.

'You've made this space special,' he said, and saw the colour rise in her cheeks again.

'I did it first—I needed a space in which I'd feel comfortable. You should see my bedroom!'

It was a natural enough statement but the moment it was out—hanging there in the air between them—she coloured even more deeply and moved towards the bookshelves, pulling out a book which she showed to Hamish.

'This is an old book of mine about possums,' she told him, resolutely ignoring Angus. 'Would you like to borrow it?'

Of course Hamish would, which meant there'd be yet another thing to return. But Hamish and Juanita could return the book; he, Angus, was out of here. Since the bedroom remark all the sensations kissing Kate had generated were returning and he was becoming more and more aware that his libido was completely out of control. Keeping out of her life was the only answer. He had to get it into his thick skull that she was a work colleague, nothing more!

'See, Dad, see,' Hamish was saying, showing him the possum on the cover of the book.

'That's great,' Angus managed, then he glanced at Kate. 'But we really must be going. Kate wants to have a shower.'

Work colleague, work colleague!

'Thanks for returning the keys,' she said, not refuting her need to have a shower or urging them to stay. 'I'll see you back at work on Monday. Here, you can go out through the front door.'

She brushed past him, out of the study and down the passage to the door, which she opened, then stepped back. He'd have liked to think it was because she didn't want to stand too close to him—that her hormones were as active as his libido—but she could also have been saving them from the weird chemical smell of stripped wallpaper and, either way, all she was, was a work colleague after all.

By Monday the baby girl, Bethany Walker, who had been admitted on Friday night, was judged strong enough to have the necessary operation. Alex had decided he would do it, but had asked Kate to act as anaesthetist. She didn't know whether to be delighted because it saved her the uneasiness of working closely with Angus that day or to be disappointed because she *wouldn't* be working closely with Angus that day! Talk about confused!

'Howdy, neighbour.'

She was in Theatre, setting out all the things she'd need, checking and rechecking drugs and equipment, when Angus walked in.

'Are you looking for Alex?' she asked, dismayed to find the zing was right here in Theatre, in the area of their workplace where it was least expected—and most inappropriate.

'No, I like to check things out before an op,' he replied, showing no evidence of zing at all.

'But Alex is doing the op,' she protested—one-way zing was the pits.

Angus smiled at her which certainly didn't help.

'And I'm assisting,' he told her cheerfully. 'I

might be okay with TGAs but the man's a genius when it comes to TAPVR, so I'd welcome any opportunity to see him at work or work with him as I will today. Is Clare our perfusionist?'

Angus wasn't sure why he'd asked the question, except that, although he was usually totally focused on his job when he was in Theatre, today he was feeling all the manifestations of the attraction his body had developed towards Kate's. He'd already decided after their strained conversation the previous day that he'd have to find a diversion. His next decision had been that he would ask Clare to have a drink with him one night or maybe dinner—go to a movie. He'd discovered back when they'd lunched together, that she was as new to Sydney as he was, and as friendless.

Kate hadn't answered his question, although she had shrugged her shoulders, so maybe she didn't know, or was she so intent in fiddling with syringes and cannulae and drugs that she hadn't heard him? He doubted that, although she may have been as determined to ignore him as he was to avoid her. He finished checking the instrument tray and left the theatre, switching his mind firmly to the operation ahead.

It went smoothly, Angus opening the little chest, spreading the ribs apart so Alex could get best access to the heart. The switch to the bypass machine went without a hitch and Alex's skill at separating out the wayward veins and reattaching them was, as far as Angus was concerned, a marvel to behold.

'Off pump!'

Alex gave the order and the whole team watched the tiny pale heart, willing it to beat, but it lay there, flat and flaccid while tension spread like noxious gas through the room.

'We'll have to shock her,' Alex said quietly, while Angus was already giving orders to Kate for the drugs the baby needed. Tension tightened but neither drugs nor electric current could restart the little heart. Angus had his hand in the baby's chest, his fingers oh-so-gently massaging it to keep blood circulating to the vital organs. Alex fired more quiet orders for different drugs, shocked again, to no avail, and Angus slid his hand back into place and continued massaging.

It was third time lucky. The third time the electric current hit the little heart it jolted; it heaved, then, rapidly at first, began to beat.

'Not arrhythmia, not now,' Alex muttered under his breath, because arrhythmia would mean more shocks, but while the whole team waited and watched, the beating steadied and a muted cheer went up. Little Bethany had made it—this far at least.

'Do you want to close or leave it open?' Angus asked Alex, and Kate held her breath. Leaving the chest open, covered only by a dressing, would mean Alex was anticipating more trouble.

'Close,' Alex said, and Kate imagined everyone let out a sigh.

'She's a little fighter,' Grace murmured, but the rest of the team grew silent, too shocked by the near loss to be chattering. Alex left the theatre; a resident, under Angus's watchful eyes, would close the chest, leaving in place drains and a pacemaker to keep the heartbeat steady. Like Bob,

Bethany would be on a ventilator for a few days at least, watched over night and day in the special PICU.

Kate waited while the baby was transferred to a crib, then followed as it was wheeled to the PICU. But as Alex was there talking to the parents, she didn't stay, thinking she'd change and return in a short while to check on her charge. But once in the changing room she slumped onto a bench, feeling as if all her energy had been drained away by the tension they'd endured in Theatre.

Angus came and sat beside her, not speaking, just sitting, yet the bulk and warmth of his body, close to hers, was infinitely comforting.

'Why do we never expect those things to happen?' she asked him. 'Why is it always such a gut-wrenching shock?'

She didn't really expect him to answer, so was surprised when, after his usual thoughtful pause, he said, 'It's the optimism thing again. If you consider it seriously, how often do we have dramas during an op? Perhaps not as dramatic as today's, but small dramas?'

Kate thought about it, then had to agree.

'Nearly every operation,' she admitted. 'A bleed, a blood vessel that kinks, unexpected difficulty getting the patient on bypass—I guess there's always something to keep us on our toes.'

She sighed and shook her head, not comforted at all.

'So why was today different?' he asked.

She turned towards him.

'Because that baby died,' she told him bluntly. 'And for a little while it looked as if she might have stayed dead! That's not why we operate, for babies to die.'

Had her voice quavered? Had her eyes filled with tears? She knew she was emotional but didn't realise she'd let it show until Angus put his arm around her and hugged her to him.

'Did they all die, your family, that you need a new one? Was it more than your sister that you lost?'

His voice was so gentle, so full of understanding, that she let out the sob she'd been holding in her chest, then, realising where she was—and who was holding her—she pushed away, swiping tears from her face.

'Oh, for Pete's sake, Angus, don't encourage me to be maudlin. I can do that well enough on my own.'

'And here I was thinking you were an optimist,' he teased, and once again she saw a glimmer of a smile in his eyes.

I could fall in love with a smiling Angus.

The thought hit her like a hammer blow.

'Well, I am.' She spoke firmly and just as firmly moved away from him, stripping off her outer layer of theatre clothes and pulling on a white coat so she'd look professional even if she was feeling like a teenager on the threshold of love.

It couldn't possibly be love. It was attraction and tension, two powerful forces combining to throw her normal commonsensical self into turmoil.

'See you later,' she said to the man causing all the trouble. He was still sitting on the bench, not smiling now, but no less attractive.

'When later?' he asked as she was about to flit through the door, hurrying away from him.

She turned back, frowning now.

'Sometime, any time—it was just a phrase, like "goodbye,"' she grumbled at him.

'Only it wasn't goodbye,' he reminded her, watching her closely, something in that regard making her stomach uneasy again.

'It's an Australian goodbye. We say it all the time—"see you later"—it doesn't mean anything.' And in case he didn't get the message, she slipped a touch of sarcasm into her voice as she added, 'And much as I'd like to stay and discuss the vagaries and variations of the English language with you, I really have to go and check on Bethany.'

He nodded, then as she shot through the door she heard him say, 'I'll see you later,' and the shiver that slithered down her spine suggested he wasn't using the words as a farewell but as a promise.

Angus knew he should stir himself from the bench. He had a cardiac catheterisation on a teenager to do and patients to check before that, but he couldn't bring himself to move, his mind turning over the totally inane conversation he'd had with Kate.

Although the earlier conversation hadn't been inane. She hadn't answered his question about her family, but the great gulp of grief she'd given had spoken for her.

'Ah, Angus, just the man I want to see.' He turned to find Clare had joined him in the changing room. 'Have you heard about this hospital social they're having on Friday night? Apparently it's to welcome all the new staff, and as I hate walking into something like that on my own, I wondered if you'd mind if we went together. We could grab an early bite to eat at that little restaurant down the road, then walk up to the hospital from there.'

Angus stared at the woman he'd been thinking he should ask out to divert his mind, not to mention his body, from thoughts of Kate, but now that she was here, asking *him* out, he didn't have a clue how to reply.

Except—

'*This* Friday?' he asked.

Clare nodded.

'Becky's put up a notice in our staff lounge.'

'I'm on call,' Angus told her, although he knew that was no excuse to not go to the shindig. After all, from the way Clare spoke, it must be being held at the hospital.

She raised her eyebrows, letting him know she knew he was prevaricating.

Feeling remarkably stupid, he rushed in to the breech. 'Of course I can go with you,' he said, then he shrugged. 'It's just that in the past I've tried to avoid hospital social activities. We spend so much time on the job as it is, it's always seemed unnecessary to return to the place when I don't have to.'

'But it *is* a way for the team to get to know one another better and for us to meet some of the hospital staff from other disciplines,' Clare pointed out. 'With Christmas only a month away, surely it's a good idea to get to know a few people.'

'Christmas!' Angus muttered. 'I keep forgetting about Christmas—I suppose because it's so darned hot it doesn't feel like November. I'd thought I might get home to Scotland this year for Christmas, until Alex pointed out that he likes to take on new staff in November, so everyone is settled in and able to cover for one another over the holiday period.'

'Believe me,' Clare said, 'this is easier than it used to be when staff were transferred from hospital to hospital at the start of a new year. You'd arrive in some country town you'd never heard of, and be thrown into New Year's Day hangovers, and fights and family break-ups all brought on by too much heat and too much alcohol. And that's not to mention the holiday road toll and all the car accidents we'd get.'

Angus studied Clare while she explained all this, seeing her lips move, her eyes sparkle, aware of how very beautiful she was, and wondering why that beauty failed to spark even a murmur of attraction in his body.

'So, Friday? Early dinner at Scoozi's? That suit you?'

Why on earth was he so reluctant? This was exactly what he needed—a woman and a beautiful one at that—to take his mind off Kate Armstrong.

'Providing I've not been called out,' he said, then it struck him that this was still far from organised. 'I haven't a car as yet so I can't offer to collect you,' he said, and she laughed.

'I just live down the road,' she said. 'I'm renting a small flat from Annie Attwood's father— Alex's father-in-law. He's in a wheelchair so he has the ground floor and he's turned the upstairs part of the house where Annie lived into two flats. Oliver's in the other one.'

Oliver's in the other one and you're asking me to walk into the social affair with you? It didn't make sense to Angus and he found himself asking her.

'Is Oliver not going?'

To Angus's surprise a faint blush coloured Clare's cheeks. Not a patch on Kate's blushes but a blush nonetheless.

'I'm not sure,' she said, and that was that.

Clare went through to the showers and Angus pulled off his theatre gear and dressed, moving quickly because he'd already wasted too much time mooning about in the changing room.

Mooning?

Definitely mooning! He could hear his mother's voice, not scolding but chiding him. You're mooning about again, she used to say, back when he was a teenager. Is it a girl?

This time it is, Mum, and I don't know what to do about it

He sent the silent message to her, not that she could help, but admitting there was some mooning to be done over the Kate situation made him feel a little better.

And having a date with Clare for Friday night—well, surely that was a good thing.

CHAPTER SEVEN

IT TURNED into one of the busiest weeks Kate could remember, and although the two babies she saw as special, Bob and Bethany, continued to do well, it seemed everything else that could go wrong did. A child showed an allergic reaction to a drug he'd had before; a young teenage girl went into arrhythmia as they were feeding a wire through her veins to take photos in her heart. Problems they overcame but which left all those involved in the procedures with tightened tension.

Or was her higher-than-usual sense of anxiety caused by the fact that she was working so closely with Angus?

Not that he showed the slightest interest in her outside professional courtesy. It was as if, as far as he was concerned, the kisses had never happened. So why were they imprinted on Kate's lips? Imbedded deep in her mind?

She hoped she was showing as cool an exterior as he was, but she doubted that was possible, knowing how her body warmed whenever he was near her.

Maybe an affair would be okay....

But even as the insidious thought slid into her mind, she felt the heaviness of loss within her body—the loss of the baby she'd never carry, never hold in her arms, because if she fell in love with Angus, how could she ever marry someone else?

If she fell in love with Angus?

She was thinking about this as she mooched home on Friday afternoon. She'd left work a little earlier than usual, wanting to wash her hair—no easy task with its curls and length—before the social do that evening.

'You're early—it's not ready yet.'

Hamish's voice, ripe with accusation, greeted her. It seemed to be coming from behind the yellow sofa which she really had to move before the summer storms began and the old wreck of a thing became saturated and smelly with mould and who knew what else.

She peered behind it to find her small neighbour busy digging a hole.

'What's not ready yet?'

'My wombat hole.'

Kate smiled to herself. Hamish always managed to make the most ridiculous things sound rational.

'And why do you need a wombat hole?'

He looked up at her now, blue eyes gleaming with excitement in a dirt-streaked face.

'So a wombat can come and live in it, of course.'

'Of course,' Kate responded weakly, sinking onto the sofa and wondering if having children was as good an idea as she'd thought it would be. Imagine having three who all wanted to dig wombat holes?

'And why are you in my front yard when it's off limits to you?' she asked.

He kept digging, although he did turn partially

towards her as he said, 'Juanita knows I'm here. I couldn't be digging it in the backyard because the wombat wouldn't see it there.'

Kate had to chuckle, picturing a large wombat strolling down the road in search of a hole, checking out front yards as it went.

'Did you have a story about wombats at kindy today?' she asked the small digger.

He shook his head, then sat back on his heels.

'Juanita bought me a book about one,' he explained. 'It's like the possum book only about a wombat so she knew I'd like it. She gave it to me because Dad's going out tonight. He won't be able to read my bedtime story, so she read it to me this afternoon when I had my rest.'

There was a lot of information in Hamish's words but the ones that stuck with Kate were 'Dad's going out tonight.'

To the hospital social?

That's where she was going, but mainly because her friend Marcie, a paediatric physician, would be there and it was some time since they'd connected.

But Angus hadn't mentioned he was going....

Why should he?

'You could help me dig if you wanted to.'

The digger had straightened up and was peering hopefully at her over the back of the sofa.

'I don't think so,' she said, switching her mind from the father to the child. 'In fact, come and sit beside me and I'll tell you some stuff about wombats.'

He came obediently enough and snuggled onto the sofa beside her.

'Do you know some wombats?' he asked.

She had to smile.

'Not personally,' she told him, 'but that's because they're not like possums. They don't live in the city, but out in the country. Wombats move very slowly, which means that if they lived in the city they'd be run over by cars or buses, so they stay way out in the country, although there are wombats in our wonderful zoo. Maybe one day your father will take you to the zoo. You can go on a ferry across the harbour, and that's fun, to see all the animals there.'

'Will you come, too?' he asked, snuggling closer, and she couldn't resist putting her arm around him and cuddling him against her, smelling dirt and sweat and little-boy smell.

'Come where, too?'

Kate closed her eyes and shook her head. One soppy cuddle with a little boy and she was caught. Hamish scrambled away from her.

'To the zoo to see a wombat. See, Dad, I made a hole for one, but Kate says he won't come because wombats don't like living in the city so I'll have to go to the zoo to see one.'

'Wombats?'

Angus had vaguely heard of such creatures, picturing in his mind something large and cumbersome, but his mind wasn't working as well as it should be, having taken off at a tangent when he'd walked down the road to see his son cuddled in Kate's arms.

His first reaction had been anxiety—Hamish had been hurt—but his son's bright voice dispelled that; the pair had been sharing nothing more than a hug.

While they talked about wombats?

He knew he was frowning but he couldn't pin down the cause for his inner uneasiness. Surely it couldn't be jealousy that Kate had achieved such closeness with Hamish so quickly? Fortunately Hamish's piping voice broke into his confusion.

'Can she, Dad, can she?'

Can she, what?

Before Angus had his mind straightened out again, Kate had answered for him.

'I've already seen them, Hamish, many times, and now I have to get inside. Stuff to do.'

She stood so hurriedly Angus knew she was escaping, not from Hamish but from him.

So she, too, was feeling confusion over the kisses they had shared. He wasn't sure if that made things better or worse as far as he was concerned, so he lifted his son off the sofa and set him on his shoulders, carrying him back to the house, letting Hamish's flow of conversation about wombats, Kate and zoos flow over and around him, anchoring him back in his real life—the father of this lad.

Father!

Again the knowledge of the wall between them raised its head, although now he considered it, it seemed, since coming to Australia, he'd been able to grow closer to his son. He'd certainly been able to look at his face—so like his mother's—without the oppressive guilt he'd once felt.

Make no mistake, the guilt still lingered—it would never go away—but it had lessened in its intensity and for that he was sincerely grateful, so much so as he set Hamish down on the floor, he hugged the little boy and whispered that he loved him.

Kate slipped her high-heeled sandals into a soft silk bag and slid her feet into flatties. She might not mind the walk to and from the hospital but in killer heels? No way! Although looking at herself, she hoped she wouldn't meet Angus on the way. The sexy black dress she'd bought for another hospital function, then been too cowardly to wear, was just fine, but with the flat shoes? No, it didn't work; it needed the high heels to set it off.

And just why was she thinking of sexy dresses
and Angus in the same breath? Wasn't she avoiding Angus? Wasn't she determined *not* to have
an affair with him? Isn't that what she'd decided
as she'd washed her hair and spent a good hour
straightening it, taming it into a shining auburn
curtain that fell to her shoulders in long, obedient
strands.

Even in the flat shoes she looked pretty good,
but—

She shook her head, making the curtain of hair
fly around her face. There was no way she could
go to a hospital function dressed like this. Oh,
she usually made some effort to look good, but
a sexy black dress, killer heels *and* straightened
hair? Her colleagues would be abuzz with specu-
lation over which new member of the team she
was trying to attract.

Sighing deeply, she pulled off the dress, but
she was damned if she'd mess with her hair.
She hauled her faithful black slacks out of the
wardrobe and found a slinky black singlet top to
go with them. It was hot enough to go with just

that, but it was a trifle bare for a casual social at the hospital, so she dug around until she found a short-sleeved cardigan, black with silver threads through it, and used it to finish her outfit. No need for high-heeled sandals, the flatties would do.

As flat as her mood, she realised as she trudged up the road towards the hospital, no longer fearing she'd run into Angus. She felt thoroughly dispirited, in fact; although dispirited didn't begin to describe how she felt when, in the foyer of the staff elevators, she ran into Angus and Clare, obviously together.

It's a good thing, she told herself, but the pain in her chest gave lie to the assertion.

Was he staring at her? Angus hoped not, but he knew his eyes continued to be drawn in Kate's direction, for all that he was responding to Clare's conversation and listening as the two women exchanged greetings.

'Your hair looks great,' Clare was saying, and Angus found himself echoing the compliment, barely refraining from adding, All of you looks great.

'Thanks.' Kate's response took in both of them, although she was looking towards Clare. 'It takes such an age to straighten it, I don't do it often.'

Was it just the hair, or was it the slim but shapely body snugly encased in black that had him all but panting like a dog?

The elevator doors opened and he stood back as Kate and Clare entered, the pair of them engrossed in what he took to be a hair conversation, as Clare was tossing her dark locks while Kate smoothed hers down against her shoulders.

'Are you with us?'

Clare asked the question and if he'd been honest he'd have had to answer no, for his thoughts were bounding all over the place, which made it very difficult for his brain to control his wayward body. But he stepped into the elevator, being careful to stand closer to Clare than Kate, but even in a large-size hospital elevator he was still too close to the woman who was disrupting his life.

It probably wasn't her fault, he'd just decided, when she brushed against him as she exited the elevator and his body went into a spasm of such hot desire he wondered if he could plead a sudden terrible headache and go home.

'Come on!' Clare was sounding impatient and he realised Kate had already entered the big room on an upper level of the hospital, while Clare was waiting patiently at the door.

Because she wants someone to see her coming in with me.

In one way the realisation was a relief, signalling as it did that Clare had no interest in him as a man, merely as a partner for this occasion. So he needn't feel guilty about the way he'd stared at Kate.

He joined Clare and together they entered the room, her hand slipping into the crook of his arm as they came towards a small cluster of their colleagues, both of them ducking to avoid some dangling Christmas decorations.

'Bloody tinsel! This close to Christmas I might have known they'd have tinsel everywhere,' Clare muttered, then she was smiling and greeting the team members, leaving Angus at a loss about the tinsel conversation.

Not that it preoccupied him for long, for there, just beyond this particular cluster of people, was Kate, the light shining on her fine white skin, and picking up the deep auburn colours in her hair. Somehow he made conversation with Alex and Oliver, smiled at a joke Becky made about doctors, then, with Clare fully occupied, he slid away, taking a drink from a tray a waiter held out, hoping his colleagues would think thirst had made him leave the group.

Deciding it would look bad if he made a beeline for Kate, he took a complete circuit of the room to get around to where she had been standing, but by the time he got there, she was gone.

'Hi, I'm Marcie, I'm a paediatric physician. You're one of the new cardiac surgeons, I believe.'

He introduced himself to Marcie, then left the conversational ball in her hands as he looked around for Kate.

'I know you worked in the U.S., but you're obviously Scottish. I did my paediatric training in Edinburgh. Did you train there at any time?'

Angus rattled off the salient points of his educational CV, and managed to hold a reasonable conversation with the woman, but apparently it wasn't reasonable enough, for finally Marcie said, 'If you're looking for Kate, she's over at the buffet. A tip for you for the future—any do like this, that's where you'll find her. She says it's because she doesn't like food that's been lying around too long so she gets in early. But, in fact, it's probably because she doesn't look after herself properly, always too busy doing something else—minding other people's children, working on her renovations or helping someone out somewhere. So she forgets to shop and forgets to eat until she's starving, then there's nothing in the fridge or pantry.'

Marcie's explanation finally ran down, but it left Angus not only with a fuller picture of his neighbour but also with a strong urge to be the one who *did* look after Kate. After all, if she didn't look after herself, someone would have to!

He was about to head towards the buffet, which he could see set up in a side room, when Clare reclaimed him.

'Let's go get something to eat,' she said, and although Angus had seen her demolish a dish of pasta that would set a footballer back on his heels, he was happy enough to go along with her—very happy, in fact.

Ha! So maybe Oliver was the focus of Clare's interest, Angus decided, checking out the crowd around the buffet and seeing only Kate and Oliver from their team. Kate and Oliver very close together, heads bent as they discussed something, Kate smiling at the man—

'Well, hi, you two—fancy meeting you here.'

Clare breezed up to them, tugging Angus by the hand until he came alongside. He knew Kate had taken in the linked hands but her expression told him nothing, which in itself was weird as Kate's face usually showed every emotion, if only in the variation of colour in her cheeks. But then, he was keeping his own reaction in check—the reaction he'd felt deep in his gut when he'd seen her with Oliver. Ridiculous, that's what it was. Apart from a couple of kisses, there was nothing between him and Kate, so why shouldn't she be standing close to Oliver?

And standing close didn't mean interest—wasn't he, Angus, standing close to Clare?

Not comfortably close, he had to admit that, although the crush now gathering around the buffet made it hard to move apart.

'Well, I'm taking my supper up on the roof,' Kate announced.

'Up on the roof? Isn't it off limits? Isn't that where the helicopter landing pad is?'

Kate smiled at him—more gut reaction.

'You haven't had the guided tour of the hospital, have you?' she said. 'There are two towers, linked on the odd-numbered floors with walkways. The helipad is on the top of the other tower. At the top of this tower, there's a wonderful roof garden, thanks to a television gardening show that did makeovers. Someone suggested that as the new buildings had taken up most of the grounds which once surrounded Jimmie's, we should have a garden on a roof. It's wonderful.'

She included all of them in her smile this time. 'Why don't we all go up?'

Was she mad, going up onto the roof with Angus? Even with the others present wasn't there a danger inherent in being out in the moonlight with him? Wandering a shadowy garden with Angus?

Although Clare seemed to have Angus firmly in hand, Kate reminded herself, to stop the mental questioning of her sanity.

'Won't it be windy up there?' Clare objected. 'It'll blow your hair.'

Kate shrugged. Clare had just offered her the perfect excuse to avoid the combination of moonlight, shadows and Angus, but she was too twitchy to stay here, making polite conversations with colleagues while the most beautiful woman in the hospital flirted with Angus. At least on the roof she might not notice Clare flirting!

'I'd like to see the roof garden.' Angus, who'd been putting two small appetisers on his plate, turned back to them to make this statement.

'Well, I'll keep an eye on Clare while you're

gone,' Oliver said, far too heartily, some false note ringing in the words. But Kate had no time to be thinking about Oliver and heartiness or false notes, for it seemed as if she and Angus were headed for the roof garden, his hand clasped on her elbow as if to ensure she didn't escape.

There'd be other people up there, she reminded herself, *and you've got a plate full of food to eat, so it isn't as if you'll have time for kisses, not that he'd be wanting to kiss you if he'd come with Clare.*

Muddled thoughts popped in and out of her mind as they walked to the elevators, but once on the roof Kate realised her assumption that other people would be about was wrong. It was obviously too early for people to be slipping away from the party.

She chose a stone seat out of the wind—Clare had been right—and began to eat while Angus deposited his plate beside her, then prowled away, obviously intent on exploring this secret wonder.

'It's wonderful,' he declared, returning as she

finished the last of the food she'd chosen and was eyeing off his meagre selection.

'It is,' she agreed, but looking at Angus, hearing the enthusiasm in his voice, she felt a pain so deep she could barely breathe.

He stood there in the moonlight, tall and strong, his accent making magic of his words—prosaic words like soil and ferns and watering systems—and she knew that it was love. Oh, people would argue that love didn't happen like this—in such a short time—but attraction, no matter how strong, couldn't cause pain as intense as she was feeling.

Her mind was battling this new revelation, but she knew sitting like a statue while it assimilated it was going to look odd, so she moved, picking up Angus's plate and helping herself to his appetisers.

'Do help yourself,' he said as she popped the second one in her mouth. 'I ate earlier.'

She looked up at him, stricken by her behaviour.

'Oh, I'm sorry, I wasn't thinking. I'll go down and get you some more.'

She stood so hurriedly she almost stumbled into him, and though she was sure he'd only put his hand on her shoulder to steady her, somehow she found herself in his arms, the plate she was still holding squashed between them.

'And waste this moonlight?'

He bent his head towards her and she could feel his lips—feel the kiss—before his mouth met hers.

'Angus, we can't!' she wailed, and heard the anguish in her voice.

He must have heard it, too, for he straightened.

'No, you're right. It's a work function and it's far too early for people to be returning to it looking rumpled and well-kissed.'

That hadn't been what she'd meant but it had stopped the kiss, which was a good thing.

Yeah?

Of course it was a good thing!

The two parts of her brain were arguing again,

but as Angus had taken the plate from her hands, put it with the other one and was striding towards the elevators, she had little alternative but to follow.

Striding?

He was angry?

With her, for stopping the kiss?

Well, he's the one that actually stopped it *and* rationalised it!

Angus pressed the button, then felt a surge of fury that the doors didn't immediately open.

Fury!

What was wrong with him, striding off like that?

Feeling anger?

And with whom, himself or Kate?

Not Kate—it wasn't her fault he felt this almost uncontrollable urge to kiss her whenever she was within a yard of him.

Nor was she to blame that she had enough sense to pull back from the kiss!

She'd joined him by the elevator, not speaking,

just standing there—within the dangerous one-yard zone but not by much.

The anger dissolved as quickly as it had surfaced, leaving him feeling confused and—

No, it couldn't be vulnerable.

He didn't do vulnerable.

'How did Hamish's mother die?'

Darn the woman! Had she sensed something? Slid inside him and ferreted out doors he'd slammed shut years ago? Somehow eased one open?

Yet might it not be time?

Around them a cool breeze rustled the leaves of the ferns and palms on the rooftop, and the scent of some sweet-smelling flower perfumed the air.

'Could we go and sit awhile?' he suggested, just as the elevator arrived and the doors opened.

Kate turned towards him, concern causing a small frown on her smooth forehead.

'You don't have to answer that question,' she said. 'In fact, it was rude and intrusive of me to have asked it, but as Hamish regards me as a friend, I thought—well, I wouldn't want to say the wrong thing to him.'

The inner tension that had eased when Kate asked the question tightened again. She was asking for Hamish, not out of concern for the boy's father.

The elevator doors had closed so he turned away, back towards the stone seat on which she'd been sitting earlier. He set down the plates on the end so she could sit beside him.

If she followed.

She did, although caution or regret was making her drag her steps.

'It's best you know,' he agreed when she slid onto the seat, close enough to touch, but not close enough for him to feel her body's warmth.

Angus looked straight ahead to where, between the branches and leaves, he caught glimpses of light in high-rise towers in the city. He'd told the story often enough, not regularly but from time to time, to explain to a colleague usually.

Kate was a colleague. Think that way!

'Jenna's pregnancy was unremarkable—she

was well throughout, and her labour was hard but not overly prolonged. She was a doctor, like myself, so one would think if she'd had any preliminary signs of deep vein thrombosis—pains in her calves, tenderness on touching—she would have said, but she was blissfully happy, keeping Hamish close, showing him off to relatives and friends.'

His voice was flat, all emotion ironed out of it by the strength of his will, but Kate knew he must be reliving that pain, and slid closer, reaching out to take his hand in hers and hold it tightly.

He didn't resist but nor did his fingers respond to hers, simply lying limp in her hand as he continued.

'You'd know that DVT is often a forerunner to a pulmonary embolism, and Jenna knew that, as well, but if she was feeling breathless or had any other symptoms she didn't say. I wasn't there when she collapsed. I'd taken Hamish out to show some of my colleagues. They started anticoagulation therapy but she was dead within thirty minutes.

Ridiculous that it can take such a short time for a young, healthy woman to die.'

Kate clung tightly to his hand. What could she say? What was there so say?

I'm sorry? A useless platitude, no matter how sincere the words!

She let the moment pass in silence, offering nothing more than whatever comfort he might derive from her clasp on his hand, then knew she had to probe again, because the pain this man was carrying was like an abscess that needed to be lanced.

'You can't possibly blame yourself,' she said, guessing this was how his thinking went. 'She must have wanted a child as much as you did, and what are the chances of a post-partum death by pulmonary embolism—very small, I would guess. Less than ten per cent?'

He stood, retrieving his hand in the action, and walked away, not towards the elevator this time, but towards the railing on the side of the roof garden that looked out over the suburbs towards the sea.

Unwilling to let him get away with silence, Kate followed him, coming to stand beside him, not touching him, but close enough for him to feel her presence.

'The mind is a strange thing, Kate,' he finally said, his voice deep and harsh. 'You'd think the scientist in me could rationalise what happened, using the figures I know by heart. Once she collapsed, there was nothing anyone could have done to save Jenna. It was just one of those occurrences that pop up to remind medical people they are not gods. But the emotional part of me cannot accept that.'

He turned towards her and put his hands on her shoulders.

'So, you see, sweet Kate, that although logically I know it wasn't my fault, emotionally I feel I was to blame. If it wasn't for me, she wouldn't have been pregnant. And yes, I know it was something we both wanted—a child—but I could never go through that again, never put a woman at risk that way, never have another child.'

He wasn't saying he could never love again....

It was a strange thought to bob into Kate's head, especially as Angus was drawing her close and she knew full well there'd be no stopping this kiss. But bob into her head it did, to lie there like a tiny seed, while her body responded to the touch of Angus's mouth, to the taste of Angus on her tongue. She slid her arms around him, holding him tight, kissing him with a passion she'd never felt before, knowing in a hazy kind of way that there was no pity in it, but sympathy at least, until the kiss became so fervid her mind went blank and she gave in to the longings of her body.

CHAPTER EIGHT

VOICES broke them apart—voices that told them others had come up to enjoy the cool breeze and beautiful views of the roof garden, or maybe to steal a kiss in shadows.

Angus looked at Kate, but her head was bent, so he smoothed the ruffled hair as best he could, thinking at the time how much better he liked her wayward curls, although the beauty of this shining curtain had taken his breath away earlier.

Who was he kidding? It was Kate herself who stole his breath.

She looked up at him now and he could see she'd been quietly renewing her lipstick, although the pale pink colour did little to hide the fullness of well-kissed lips.

'I think I'll go straight home,' she said. 'No-one will think anything of it—I rarely stay long at these occasions, and I've seen the person I came to see.'

Which obviously wasn't me, Angus realised, then chided himself for feeling put out. She saw him all the time at work; she didn't need to make a special effort. And she'd been kissing him, not some other man. She was here with him—

She was here with him!

The realisation released a lot of the tension that had built up again after the kiss.

'I'll walk you home,' he said, his body already stirring in response to this brilliant idea.

Green witch eyes studied him intently.

'Aren't you forgetting something?'

'Forgetting something?' He raised his eye-brows.

'Or someone?' Kate clarified, but obviously Angus still didn't get it.

'You came with Clare,' Kate reminded him. 'Surely you should see her home.'

'Oh, but it wasn't that kind of coming with,' Angus stuttered, and Kate almost laughed, almost but not quite. It wasn't really a night to be amused by seeing the usually oh-so-together Angus all confused.

'Whatever kind of coming with it was,' she told him, 'you should at least see that she's okay to get home. Besides, as I've told you before, I'm quite capable of seeing myself home.'

She was, but as she plodded up the street, a heaviness she rarely felt descended on her spirit. Angus had been honest with her from the start— no more children in his life—but the attraction between them, the attraction she knew he felt, had swayed her into thinking maybe something could come of a relationship between them.

Swayed her into thinking maybe he'd change his mind.

But now she knew how he felt, she had to cross that, admittedly remote, possibility right out of contention.

And why was she thinking of relationships of any kind with Angus when all they'd done so far was kiss?

Honesty propelled the answer: because she wanted there to be more than kisses—she wanted a relationship. And now that she knew she loved him, the need was not just for an affair kind of relationship but one that might possibly have a future.

With no babies?

Get real, Armstrong, you're so far ahead of the play here you're out of the field. There is no relationship! Get that into your thick head and get on with your life.

He caught up with her as she turned into her gate.

'Oliver is taking Clare home,' he panted, 'which I think is what she wanted all along.'

'So?' Kate demanded, angry with her body for responding to his arrival and angry with him for disrupting her when she'd only just got things sorted in her head, and had her wayward impulses back under control.

'So, I can see you home,' he said, less puffed now so he could smile as he spoke and it was the smile that was Kate's undoing.

Not that she could let him see it.

'I am home,' she pointed out.

'But I can see you to the door,' he whispered, the words zapping along her nerves like electric currents.

He hooked his arm around her shoulders and drew her close, kicking the gate open and walking her up the short path to the shadowed porch.

If he kisses me, I'm gone.

It was Kate's last rational thought. They'd no sooner reached the porch than Angus's lips captured hers and she was swept into the maelstrom of delight just kissing Angus caused. Swept into eddying currents of desire so deep and swift she knew there was no escape.

She eased one hand out of his grasp and dug in her pocket for a key, wordlessly unlocking the door and walking in, still in his embrace, his lips now seeking other places to kiss—her temple, just below her ear and the little hollow at the base of her neck.

Every kiss provided its own erotic thrill, each different, yet building and building the desire that was already flooding through her body.

'Bedroom, I think?' he whispered, the huskiness

of his voice sending shivers down her spine, weakening the muscles in her legs.

He lifted her then, carrying her as easily as he carried Hamish, up the stairs and turning as if by instinct towards her bedroom at the front of the house.

She closed her eyes and tried not to think of the clothes scattered around on every surface, the skirt she'd worn to work probably on the floor, the sexy black dress cast aside on a chair. As long as they didn't turn on a light—

And *why* was she thinking about the disarray in her bedroom at a time like this?

She knew full well—it was to save her thinking about the consequences of what was about to happen. She was about to make love with Angus, and though the aftermath of that action might break her heart, she wanted it more than she'd ever wanted anything in her life.

Especially now Angus was kissing her again, only this time his hand was underneath her singlet, underneath her bra, touching her breast, feeling for her nipple. And pressed against her was the evidence of his desire, hard and strong, moving only slightly against her body but exciting her with the subtle movement.

She eased his shirt out of his trousers and slid her hands onto the skin on his back, feeling the silky smoothness of it, pressing her fingers into flat muscle mass and hard ribs, learning Angus through touch.

But her fingers couldn't possibly be exciting him as much as his were exciting her, for now he was cupping her breast and she could feel it grow heavy, her nipple peaking with desire, his tweaking on it sending fiery messages directly down to the sensitive nub between her thighs.

'Can we dispense with clothes?' she murmured against his chin, hoping she sounded less desperate than she felt.

'No sooner said than done,' he responded, and somehow, with hands flailing and feet moving, they stripped each other off, then came together again, skin to skin, less frantic now, savouring this moment of meeting properly, revelling in the togetherness of naked bodies.

'I grabbed some protection before I left the hospital,' Angus muttered, bending to retrieve his trousers and digging into a pocket before dropping a handful of foil-wrapped condoms on the bedside table.

'That many? What are you, the Scottish stud?' Kate teased, although the teasing was hiding her silly disappointment. Was she mad? She might want a baby but not an accidental pregnancy, especially with Angus, so why disappointment?

'You'll see,' Angus was saying as he lifted her again and tossed her lightly onto the bed, following her down so his body lay full-length beside her, on his side so he could lean towards her, touch her, kiss her, tease her with his tongue and fingers, and with words too, soft words that questioned and suggested. Their exploration of each other became a voyage of discovery until the teasing brought Kate to the very edge of orgasm and she cried out to have him deep inside her so satisfaction could be shared.

* * *

They'd used two condoms, Kate remembered that much as movement on the bed disturbed her exhausted sleep. She reached out for Angus but he was already up, dressing in the darkness.

'You're going?'

She hoped she'd sounded less desperate, less disappointed, than she felt! He sat down on the bed, and leaned over her, kissing her gently on the lips.

'I must, sweet Kate, for all I'd love to stay. But Hamish, knowing it's Saturday, will be bouncing into my bed at the crack of dawn which, in this upside-down country seems to be about 5:00 a.m.'

'Later now we're on summer time,' Kate corrected, although this totally unnecessary piece of information was nothing more than an attempt to mask the hurt she felt. Rationally she knew Angus had to get home to his son—of course he couldn't spend the night with her.

He pulled on his shoes, then bent to kiss her again, offering, as he stood, yet another piece of explanation.

'He'll be on a high because I'm taking him to the zoo to see the wombats.'

Kate waited, but the invitation she longed to hear didn't come, so she slid out of bed, pulled on a robe, fortunately slung over the bedpost nearby, and caught up with him at the door.

'There's a deadlock,' she explained, trying to sound as practical and matter-of-fact as he had. 'I'll lock the door behind you.'

She followed him down the steps, willing the idea of inviting her to the zoo with them to occur to him, but as he dropped a second goodbye kiss on her lips at the door she realised just how compartmentalised Angus's life must be. Okay, so she'd caught a glimpse inside one compartment tonight—the one labelled Jenna—but the Angus and Hamish boxes were still locked against her.

And probably always would be!

The realisation saddened her, but at least she knew where she stood and now it was up to her to decide where she wanted to fit into his life. Would she be happy to be in her own box? One marked

Kate for Sex? Well, maybe he wasn't *that* crass! Maybe it was just marked Kate!

But, loving him as she did, could she handle it? She had no idea, and standing in the dark hallway wasn't going to supply one, so she went back to bed and curled up on the side where the scent of his body still lingered, memories of their love-making carrying her back to sleep.

She'd been right about the compartmentalisation of Angus's life, she realised when, after escaping to a friend's place in the Blue Mountains for the weekend to avoid him—and to think—she was back in the company of the professional Angus.

Was it easy for him, or did he want to lean into her when they were close, as she did to him? Did he want to touch her lightly as they passed, brush his fingers against her arm or back, as her fingers ached to do to him?

There was no sign that he did, but then, life at work had been hectic and there'd been little time for social interaction of any kind. Early in the week it was fairly standard chaos, except that two theatre nurses were off with summer colds and the team was working with theatre staff they didn't know, which always made things go a little less smoothly.

And even when she had no patients to check, Kate stayed at work later than she needed to, still uncertain in her mind—though not her heart— just where she wanted to fit in Angus's ordered life. She was determined to avoid accidental contact with him until she'd worked it out.

If she worked it out!

If she was right that he compartmentalised his life, could she accept that?

Or was she wrong about his attitude?

Although he'd have had to shut off part of himself after his wife died....

Her heart hoped she was wrong, but on top of the lack of an invitation to join him and Hamish at the zoo, Angus's behaviour at work, professional to the nth degree, told her she was right. Okay, so she didn't want a cuddle in the linen closet or a quick kiss in the procedures' room, but some acknowledgement of what had happened between them—a touch, a wink, an offer of a shared coffee break—would have made her feel less insecure.

The week went from bad to worse on Thursday, when they had a baby transferred into Jimmie's with hypoplastic left heart syndrome, a bad congenital defect where the left ventricle which pumped blood into the aorta, thence all through the body, was virtually missing. Kate first met the baby, Karl Sutcliffe, when she was called in to do the anaesthesia for the investigative procedures. He was such a chubby wee infant it was hard to believe he had a severe abnormality in his heart.

'Have you been involved in many cases of HLHS?' Angus asked, and knowing he liked to have people talking as he worked, she responded.

'Only one Norwood,' she said, naming the first operation that was usually performed on newborns with the problem, 'but I've been involved with a few who've had the bidirectional shunt inserted at six months and one little girl who had a Fontan at eighteen months.'

'That's the trickiest of the three,' Angus said, carrying on the conversation, although Kate knew ninety-nine point nine per cent of his attention was on this patient. 'Connecting the superior and inferior vena cava veins to the pulmonary artery can be very tricky, especially as the lungs have to be strong enough to adapt to the change.'

'Well, Phil did that one, and it went beautifully. I saw the little girl a couple of weeks ago when she was in for a check-up and she looked great.'

'Are we talking about Lucy Welsh?' Angus asked, glancing up at Kate, the dark eyes causing tremors she shouldn't feel at work.

'That's her,' Kate responded, trying to focus solely on work. 'Is she seeing you now?'

Angus nodded. 'That's right and she's doing really well.' There was a pause before he added, 'Okay, we're all done here.'

Something in his voice made Kate look more closely at him.

'And?' she probed.

He nodded to the technician who'd been handling the equipment, asked for a number of specific prints, then, as Kate checked the baby's blood gases, he sighed and answered.

'It's worse than the X-rays, ECG and echo showed. There's no ventricle at all, and the aorta is compromised, as well.'

'You can't operate?'

Kate hoped she sounded more professional than she felt, but hearing news like this always shocked her. Without an operation this baby would die.

'I'll talk to Alex, show him what I've found, but I doubt it.'

He sounded tired and more than ever Kate longed to touch him, even a light touch on his shoulder, but Angus was in work mode and every movement he made, every glance he gave her, told her this.

Angus saw Kate flinch and longed to reach out and touch her—nothing more than a reassuring brush of his fingers—but this was work and he knew from experience he had to keep his work life separated from his personal life.

Yet he owed Kate something.

'Cup of coffee?' he suggested. 'Once you've got him hooked up back in the PICU?'

'Where?' she asked.

He glanced at his watch. It was after five, the day had got away from him.

'If you're knocking off, let's make it Scoozi's. Hamish has a playdate with a kindy friend so won't be home until late. Besides, he and Juanita are used to expecting me when they see me.'

She nodded but he sensed she wasn't over-joyed by the idea. She'd been avoiding him—he'd figured that out quickly enough—but why? Embarrassment over what had happened Friday night? Or avoidance so there'd be no chance of it ever happening again?

His body didn't like that idea, not one little bit. Kate Armstrong had excited it in ways he'd never felt before and he'd hoped she'd enjoyed the experience enough to want to continue it.

He reached the restaurant first and chose a table in the outdoor garden section. A pergola overhead shaded the area from the worst of the day's sun so it was pleasantly cool, and he sipped his coffee and found his body not only relaxing, but stirring at the thought of seeing Kate in private—or more or less private, at least not at the hospital.

'Is there nothing we can do for that baby?'

So much for his body stirring! But he didn't have to answer straightaway, did he? He stood and moved to pull out her chair.

'Sit down, relax. Do you want a coffee or a drink—a glass of wine, maybe? I know they have that white you liked.'

She stared at him as if he'd gone demented, then her lovely lips clamped together in a thin line.

'You know that because you and Clare ate here last Friday night, I assume, and no, I didn't come for a drink, but for you to talk about that baby. Isn't that why you asked me?'

Kate heard the words come flying out before she could prevent them. What was wrong with her? Here she was, meeting Angus at *his* invitation, and she was carrying on like a shrew.

'Sit,' Angus said, but gently this time, his hand offering just the slightest downward pressure to her shoulder.

Damn him! Just one touch and she was jelly! Angry jelly, although she knew full well the anger was irrational. She slumped down into the chair.

'Coffee or wine?'

His repetition of the offer made her shake her head, but maybe a glass of wine would help her through whatever lay ahead.

'Wine, please.'

He gave her order to a waiter and settled back in his chair, reaching out across the table to grasp her hands.

'Yes,' he said, 'I sensed you needed to talk about the baby, but we need to talk about other things, as well, Kate. I came over to see you on Sunday afternoon when Hamish was asleep but you weren't there, and at work, well, I—'

'Like to keep things professional,' she finished for him. 'I did guess that.'

'But do you understand it?'

Did she? Kate thought about it, pleased her wine had arrived so she could take a sip and put off replying for a moment.

'To a certain extent, but as most doctors and nurses end up in relationships with other doctors and nurses, it's usually obvious what's going on around the place. In our unit alone there've been seven relationships that I know of, and it's only been set up a couple of years.'

He shrugged, the movement of his shoulders reminding her how the skin on those shoulders had felt, reminding her of too many things.

'It happens, but for me it's easier to keep things more—'

'Compartmentalised?' Kate offered the guess she'd already made about this man.

'I suppose so,' he admitted, then he stared off into space and she knew he was either thinking of some excuse for this behaviour, or wondering if he'd tell her the real reason.

'Back when Jenna died,' he finally began, and she knew he'd come down on the side of the latter. She also felt a tiny surge of happiness that he was opening the crack in that particular box just a little wider. 'We'd both been working at the hospital, so everyone knew us—knew us as a pair.'

He paused, his eyes once again on the greenery on the far side of the garden area.

'I had to keep working there—I had a fellowship, studying under one of the best paediatric cardiac surgeons in the business.' He turned back to Kate, dark eyes pleading for something—understanding?

'It was terrible, Kate. I could cope, just, with Jenna's death. I knew I had to come to terms with it and that in time I would, but the sympathy, the commiserations, of the staff around me—everyone knowing and wanting to help—it made it so much harder.'

'So from then on you shut yourself into a box called Work and thought that would shield you from emotion? Did you never think that maybe having people around you who knew you both might be a good thing? That their empathy and understanding and friendship and even love might have helped you through that time, even if it was only in giving you something to kick against?'

He stared at her, frowning slightly.

'I didn't see it that way,' he finally replied. 'And

I still don't see it as shutting myself away in a box. I'm trying to explain that, at the time, it grated on me and I decided that I wouldn't mix my professional and private lives ever again.'

'Until you went to bed with me last Friday night!' Kate reminded him, making him frown even harder.

'But can't we keep that separate? Does everyone have to know?'

Kate shook her head, a sadness she didn't understand riffling through her senses.

'"Everyone" being hospital staff, or "everyone" being them plus Hamish and Juanita? Just how private a box do you want this relationship to be in?'

He threw up his hands.

'How do I know? You started the box thing—I don't see it like that at all!'

If he'd argued that he just wanted to keep things quiet at work, Kate knew she might have had a hope of a reasonable relationship with the man she loved, but he'd not answered the Hamish question, which hurt her more than she could say.

'Don't you?' she said. 'Okay, enough of boxes. I don't like them anyway. I like my world to be in circles, overlapping rings that encompass all I do and all the people I love. So tell me about the baby. You feel there's no hope?'

Angus stared at her, seeing the pale oval of her face against the richness of her hair—curling wildly again.

'Angus?'

Had he been silent too long? What had she asked while he'd tried to analyse a very nasty constriction in his gut? The baby!

'I'll discuss it with Alex—in fact, I'm seeing him this evening before he flies to Melbourne for a conference. But I think the best we can do is list the baby for a heart transplant and hope that one becomes available while he's still well enough to survive an operation.'

'Poor kid—poor parents. Did you speak to them?'

Angus shook his head.

'Not until I've spoken with Alex so we can present them with all the information and options—however limited those might be. I've not been here long enough to know the ins and outs of the transplant listing system, how long a donor waiting list might be, how cases are prioritised.'

He might have been talking work but as he watched Kate lift her wineglass and drain the last mouthful, he couldn't help looking at her lips, thinking of the magic they'd wrought on his body such a short time ago.

Would he ever taste them again?

He wanted to ask, to find out how she felt about continuing a relationship with him, but what could he say? Can we have sex again?

Of course he couldn't.

'This is ridiculous,' he finally blurted out. 'I'm nearly forty years of age, sitting with a woman to whom I am incredibly attracted, and I don't know how to ask her if we've got anything going between us.'

Kate stared at him, then smiled and shook her head.

'Perhaps you should have got out a bit more and learnt a little about the way of the world.'

She paused and the smile slid off her face. 'Yes, we've got something going between us, Angus. It's called attraction—a very strong attraction— strong enough for us to end up in bed together last Friday night. I've had a few days to think about it and, believe me, I did a lot of thinking. But I've always known that relationships that are simply for sex are not for me. I know they work for some people, but as far as I'm concerned, apart from the purely physical release, there's no fulfilment in them.'

Anger filtered into his head but he squashed it down. He wanted this woman in ways he didn't fully understand, and although so far in this conversation he'd done nothing more than turn her off him, he was determined to make a reasonable argument.

'You're making a judgement call on our relationship before we've even got to know each other properly. I won't accept it's just for sex. I like you, and I'd like to see more of you out of hospital hours. Are you afraid of what might happen? Are you afraid it might turn into a deeper relationship than you can handle? Is that why you're dodging it?'

'*I'm* dodging it? That's a laugh!

But although she'd snapped the argument at him, Kate knew he was right. Of course that was why she was dodging it. Because at the end, whatever happened, it wasn't going to lead to the family she had craved for so long.

So instead, she'd forgo any pleasure the relationship could provide? What if a grandfather for her grandchildren *never* came along?

'I don't know,' she finally admitted, her head and heart so at war with each other she felt exhausted.

'"I don't know" will do me for the moment,' Angus said, his tone exultant. 'Now, I'm meeting Alex at his house so I'll walk you home through the park. You are going home?'

She nodded, though walking home through the park was the last thing she wanted to do. The park was special to her, a favourite place, and she didn't want it tainted by the uneasiness she was feeling with Angus.

'You said the house where you live had been your family home, so you grew up with the park as a playground?'

Had he read her thoughts? They were on the path that led directly across it towards the street where they lived. It ran under spreading poinciana trees, already in bud, some showing the beginnings of the red-and-gold flowers that would shortly make a vibrant canopy overhead.

'We moved there after Susie died,' she said, not exactly answering his question.

She thought about it some more, then honesty propelled further explanation.

'Yes, I loved the park. I escaped to it as often as I could.'

'Escaped?'

She stopped by a sundial in the centre of a small piazza where several paths converged.

'You of all people would know that grief doesn't go away just because you move house,' she said. 'It came with us, and it haunted my parents' lives, so yes, I escaped to it. The park was light and sunny and even in the shadows it was warm.'

Angus felt a tension in his chest as he imagined the child Kate had been, alone with grieving parents, using the park as an escape from the darkness grief brought in its train.

Was *his* grief haunting Hamish?

He took Kate in his arms and kissed her gently on the lips, then simply held her, trying to work out the upheaval going on in his mind. He'd always put down the gap between himself and Hamish to Hamish's resemblance to his mother, but had he deliberately shut himself off from his child, as well as his colleagues?

Was Kate right about his behaviour, about his shutting himself away?

He'd have to think about it later, because right now the woman in his arms, held lightly but still held, was more important.

'Are your parents both dead now?' he asked, and she looked up at him and nodded.

'My mother died when I was eighteen. She'd been ill for a long time, or so it seemed. My father died three years ago. That's when I moved out of the house.'

'And you had no-one?'

She moved out of his embrace.

'Not really. I had someone after my mother died,' she said. 'Although probably no-one would have been better.'

The words weren't bitter but they had a hint of tartness in them, then suddenly she smiled, a proper smile, a 'Kate smile.'

'Didn't I tell you once not to make me maudlin! I had, and still have, a group of wonderful friends. I've had a great life and intend to continue enjoying it. Okay, so it had its share of bumps but all lives have their bumps. You have to live with that so you can enjoy the smooth bits all the more because of them.'

She marched off down the path so he had to hurry to catch up with her. There was more—he sensed that—more about the 'no-one' she'd probably have been better without. Not her father. A man, no doubt! No wonder she was wary about a relationship with him.

But wasn't he just as wary?

Wanting to keep it quiet?

Wasn't that unfair?

Belittling her some way?

He rubbed his hands through his hair, aware his mind was more confused than it had ever been. *His* mind, the mind he prided himself could work through any problem.

They walked in silence, crossing the road together, then parting without farewells, he to see Alex in the house further down the street, she to disappear into her house.

'So *that* has done a lot of good!' he muttered to himself as he walked through Alex's front gate.

'Talking to yourself, Angus?'

He looked up to see Alex's wife, Annie, heavily pregnant with their second child and positively radiant, cutting roses in the front garden.

And in his mind's eye he saw not Jenna but a pregnant Kate, and the image shocked him so much he stopped as if he'd hit a telegraph pole.

'Incipient madness!' he said to Annie.

'Comes with the job, I think,' she said sympathetically. 'Go on in, I think Alex is doing something about cold drinks.'

In a corner of the big living room a toddler played with coloured blocks, knocking over the towers Alex was building for him, then gnawing at random blocks.

'He's teething,' Alex explained, standing up to greet Angus. 'But then they always are, it seems. You'd know about it.'

Another stab of guilt. *Had* he known much about Hamish's developmental milestones? He supposed his mother had told him when teeth came through, and he'd dutifully admired them, but as a father?

This was doing his head in. Thank heavens Juanita had picked up their car today. He'd talk to Alex, then head for the beach, take a walk to clear his head. He'd heard you could walk for miles along a headland path from Coogee. He'd do that—

He caught up with Alex's conversation, saying yes to a cold drink, but thinking now, as Alex disappeared to get drinks, not of a solitary walk but perhaps a trip to the beach with Hamish. They could swim and play in the sand.

Ask Kate?

Not this time, there was a lot of catching up to do, but soon he'd ask Kate—

Ask Kate what?

CHAPTER NINE

'I HATE transplants.'

They were in Theatre. Oliver was preparing baby Karl. Angus was to do the operation as Alex was still in Melbourne, but it was Clare who voiced the emotion Kate also felt.

'Why?' Oliver asked as he cut open the tiny chest of the patient.

'For me it's because some other baby has to die.' It was Kate who answered. 'I know it means this baby will live, and one lot of parents will have the joy, but I always think of the other parents, the ones going home with empty, aching arms, and bruises on their hearts that will last for ever.'

'Just slightly melodramatic, Kate?' Angus had returned from speaking to the patient's parents in time to hear her words.

'I don't think so,' she said, barely glancing at

Angus, who'd been avoiding her assiduously since their coffee and walk through the park a week earlier. Although, to be fair, with Alex away, Angus was busier than usual.…

She'd been avoiding him, as well, although she'd seen plenty of Hamish, who, having been reunited with McTavish, was spending a lot of time adventuring in her backyard.

But when Angus spoke again, she was startled and just a little put out, for he was opening the box that was Jenna, not just to her but to his colleagues.

'My wife died suddenly,' he was saying, while Kate tried to concentrate on her job and ignore the emotion bumbling around in her chest. 'As a physician, she'd always been an advocate of organ donation, yet at the time of her death, when a woman from the organ donor program approached me, all I felt was revulsion. I was about to refuse when I remembered how vocal Jenna had been about it, and although it ripped me apart at the time, I agreed that they should take whatever they could use.'

He paused, and the normal sounds of the operating theatre seemed louder in his silence, then he added, 'But it does bring comfort later, when you can think more clearly, and to parents of a child that died to know their child didn't die in vain, I think that must, in time, be helpful.'

Kate stared at him, and though his dark eyes, all but hidden behind the magnifying loupe, turned her way, she could read nothing in them. Yet she sensed that this was probably the first time Angus had spoken openly to colleagues about his wife's death, and wondered if perhaps this, too, would be helpful to him.

Her love for him made her want to go to him, to put her arms around him and hold him tightly, but this was work, and here in this place, they were colleagues and nothing more.

Perhaps that's all they were anywhere; nothing had been resolved....

The talk around the operating table was purely professional now, with the circulating nurse offering the latest information on the expected arrival time of the donor heart, the operating team counting down the minutes, preparing precisely, so little Karl's time on the machine would be as short as possible. And as the operation proceeded, Kate lost her reservations about transplants. Angus did the switch so swiftly it seemed impossible to think dozens of tiny stitches had been inserted as the new heart was set in place and connected to Karl's blood vessels, but now, as the heart beat on its own for the first time in Karl's chest, Kate felt the joy that *this* baby had survived.

Angus was in the PICU with Karl's parents when she and Clare wheeled the baby through. Clare was really in charge now he was on the ventilator, but Kate wanted to see him settled before she left the hospital.

And not only was Angus with the parents, but he had his arm around Karl's mother, who had tears welling in her eyes as she thanked him and his team.

'You've humanised me again, Kate Armstrong,' he told her later, catching up with her as she walked through the early-evening light along their street. 'And for that I thank you.'

He slung an arm around her shoulder and drew her close.

'I'm not saying you were right about the boxes, mind,' he added, 'but I'd lost my way and now I see a faint hint of a path ahead of me.'

Which meant what? Kate wondered but didn't ask, simply enjoying the feel of his arm around her, the solidity of his body against hers.

'So, dinner tonight at Scoozi's? Or somewhere else if you'd prefer? I don't know the places to go so you choose.'

Kate shook her head, remembering another conversation—dinner and sex, a movie and sex...

'Why?' she asked, perhaps a little bluntly, as they reached his front gate.

'Because,' he said, and kissed her, right there and then for all the world—or any of it that happened to be around at the time—to see. 'We're starting again. I'm courting you. We're not going to get tangled up in where we're going or what might happen in the future—we're going to take it one day at a time and see what happens.'

He kissed her again.

'That suit you?'

All Kate could do was nod, too overwhelmed by the sudden change in this man to take it in. Perhaps…

'Then why don't you come to my place for dinner,' she suggested. 'That way we can get to know each other a little better than we would in a restaurant.'

A sexy smile greeted this pronouncement, and before she could protest that that wasn't what she'd meant, he was kissing her again.

'I'll read Hamish his bedtime story and be in at eight,' he promised as they drew apart, and though Kate was reasonably sure her feet were touching the ground as she made her way next door, it felt as if she was dancing at least a yard above the ground, flying like a fairy in a bright bubble of happiness.

He came, they talked, and ate, and talked some more. They wandered through the park, hand in hand, kissing in the shadows, prolonging the agony of desire for as long as they could. Then suddenly both needing more than kisses, hurrying back to her house, to her bedroom, stripping off their clothes and lying together once more, not talking now, but letting their hands renew the exploration of each other's bodies.

It was a dream yet not a dream, Kate decided as the escalation of her desire blasted thoughts of the future from her mind. For the moment there was only now, and right now, here with Angus, was where she wanted to be.

His teasing fingers brought her to a whimpering, tremulous climax, and as he slid inside her, she shivered again, knowing that she would surely splinter into a million pieces the next time. But it was Angus who cried out loud when the moment came, his body shuddering with his release, his arms clamping her to his body as if she was a lifeline in a very turbulent sea.

They lay together, Kate holding him close, knowing so much had changed in his life recently he might feel totally adrift, and as she held him, he drifted off to sleep, and she watched over him in the moonlight that streamed through her window.

Would it go anywhere, this relationship?

Did it matter if it didn't?

Couldn't she simply take what she could out of it, and if a time came to move on, then she'd have memories to treasure in the future?

But even as she assured herself this was possible, she knew that she was wrong. The more time she spent with Angus, the more she learned of his convoluted personality, the more she loved him, and the harder any parting would eventually be.

So she held him as he slept and tried not to think, simply reliving the pleasure of the evening they'd spent together—the walk in the park, the kisses under the trees, the magic of his lovemaking.

'You should have woken me!'

It was two in the morning and she was sitting up in bed, still watching over him, having decided that was far more satisfying than sleeping beside him, when he came awake so suddenly she was startled.

But the accusation in his words startled her even more, and as she watched him pull on his clothes, she felt her happiness seep away, leaving only emptiness. How had she fooled herself that Angus had changed? Why had she thought that two kisses outside his gate meant he was willing for people to know they were in a relationship?

'I would have woken you soon,' she muttered, angry now at his reaction. 'I know you like to be home before Hamish wakes.'

'I've got to go—I'll see you later. You're on call this weekend? You'll be here?'

He was out the door, doing up his shirt with one hand, his shoes and socks in his other.

Kate stared at the empty doorway, then heard him call from the bottom of the steps.

'Don't forget to come down and lock the door before you go back to sleep.'

Go back to sleep? Ha! She was so confused she might never sleep again.

Maybe he hadn't meant to be so offhand?

Who was she kidding?

Dinner and sex, movies and sex—that was

Angus's idea of a relationship and she'd known that from the start. Just because he was becoming more human in other areas of his life didn't mean he was going to fall madly in love with his next-door neighbour.

She must have slept for she was woken by a strange noise at her back door, and she pulled on a robe and made her way downstairs to find McTavish sitting on the doorstep, whimpering piteously.

'What's wrong, where's Hamish?' she asked the dog, then realised how pathetic that was.

She called the boy, thinking he must be hiding somewhere and McTavish couldn't find him, but there was no reply, and in spite of her sudden rush of anxiety a quick search of her backyard revealed no unconscious little boy.

Picking McTavish up, she was walking towards the gate when she realised she was hardly dressed for visiting.

'Come inside with me,' she told him, carrying him into the kitchen and putting some water for him into a bowl. 'I'll get some clothes on and we'll investigate.'

He sat beside the water bowl, the dark brown eyes in the pale Highland terrier face looking so sorrowful she had to hug him again before she went upstairs to change.

But going next door provided no answers. The little car Angus had bought was on the concrete pad in the backyard, but no-one was at home.

'Well, do you want to stay here or come home with me?' she asked McTavish, who put his nose against her leg by way of answer and followed her back into her yard.

'I don't have a dog door but I'll leave the back door open,' she told him, but apparently, having found one of the few humans he knew in Australia, McTavish wasn't going to budge from her side.

By late afternoon Kate was seriously worried, and although she'd phoned her neighbours frequently there was no reply, and no answering machine picked up. She'd never had reason to know Angus's mobile number and wondered about phoning the hospital and asking them to contact

Angus on his pager. But she knew how much he'd hate that, so she sat and worried, cleaned her living-room walls down and worried, took McTavish for a walk in the park using a belt for a lead, and worried.

At midnight, when McTavish's scratching at her bedclothes told her he needed to go outside, she let him out into the backyard and saw lights on next door, but they were upstairs in Juanita's flat and Kate didn't feel she knew Juanita well enough to visit her at midnight.

Instead, she tried to shoo McTavish back home, but although he went through the gate and wandered around for a while, he came back and followed Kate inside.

'Stuck with each other, aren't we?' she said, although by morning she knew she had to find out what had happened. Clutching McTavish's solid body under one arm, she went next door, to the front door this time, and pressed her finger on the bell. So what if it was barely seven; the dog was lost, well, kind of lost....

And so was she, but that was different.

Juanita came eventually. Not the cheerful, competent Juanita Kate was used to seeing, but a sleep-rumpled Juanita with dark shadows under her eyes.

'The dog! I'd forgotten all about him. He hasn't been here long enough for me to remember he's part of the family. Have you been looking after him?'

She reached out to take McTavish but Kate held on to her prize.

'What's happened?' she asked. 'He's been at my place since yesterday morning and I've tried to contact Angus any number of times.'

'You don't know?'

Juanita sounded shocked, but the look of her, and now the tone of her voice, was filling Kate with a strong foreboding.

She shook her head.

'It's Hamish!' Juanita said, her voice catching on his name, and tears welling in her eyes. 'Just suddenly on Friday night—he was sleeping in my flat because Angus was out, and he started crying, then he stopped, suddenly. One minute crying, then no crying. I went to check—he was asleep. He felt a little hot but he gets ear infections and a temperature sometimes and he was sleeping so I didn't wake him. Then in the morning—very early, it was still dark—he was going down the stairs to his own flat and he fell. Angus thought he'd knocked himself out and took him up to the hospital for X-rays but it wasn't the fall. He's got enceph—'

'Encephalitis?' Kate whispered, finishing the word that Juanita was trying to get out.

Juanita nodded.

'The doctors there say he must have had some kind of virus and this followed it, but until last night he's been well as far as we could see.'

'And Angus?'

'He is by his son's bed where he should be,' Juanita said, somehow implying it's where he should have been when Hamish was first ill. Not that Kate needed Juanita's words to make her feel guilty; she'd been feeling guilt since she'd first heard of the little boy's illness.

And if she was feeling guilt, how would Angus

be feeling—Angus who was a world champion in the guilt stakes.

She handed McTavish over and headed straight for the hospital, then had second thoughts and turned back, returning home to get her hospital ID just in case she was stopped from entering the intensive-care unit where Hamish would be.

He was in a small room, hooked up to monitors, a haggard-looking Angus by his side.

'I'll sit with him while you take a break,' she said, coming close but not touching either the man or the comatose child.

Angus looked up at her, his dark eyes almost black with worry.

And regret!

Although maybe she was imagining the regret.

'I should have been there for him earlier in the evening,' he muttered, confirming her fears that Angus would be taking on entire responsibility for his son's illness.

'He could have sickened during the day, while

you were operating, while he was at kindy—any time, Angus, and you know it.'

The dark eyes turned away from her, and though she longed to touch him, hold him, help to bear his pain, he'd erected a wall between them, so obvious she could almost see it.

'Take a break,' she said. 'I'm speaking as a doctor now, not a friend. You'll be worse than useless if you don't look after yourself and you know it.'

'He hasn't roused at all,' Angus muttered. 'They're giving him corticosteroids but there's little else they can do.'

'He knows me well enough now, Angus, for me to be with him if he does rouse, so go, if only to have a shower and get fresh clothes. Something to eat and drink.'

To her surprise Angus stood, ceding his place to her, and as she slipped into the chair he touched his hand to her shoulder.

'I'm sorry,' he said, his voice gruff with exhaustion, and although he was gone before Kate could question the remark, it filled her with a coldness she didn't want to consider.

She took Hamish's hand in hers, and talked to him, about possums and wombats and McTavish coming to visit her and staying the night, chattering on, hoping something in the stream of words might penetrate enough to rouse him. It was only when a different nurse came in to do his obs that she realised she'd been there over a change of shift, and checking her watch saw Angus had been gone two hours.

Maybe he'd had a sleep!

She was pleased for him but, stupidly perhaps, even more pleased for herself that he'd trusted her to sit with his son.

But his return, another hour later, was no cause for pleasure, his thanks spoken so brusquely Kate flinched.

'I'll stay a little longer,' she suggested, for in spite of his attitude she knew he needed support.

'There's no need,' he said, and now she did depart, stopping by the monitors to speak to the nurse in charge, a young man she knew quite well because he'd done a stint in the cardiac PICU.

'It's not good that he's not rousing,' he said. 'The swelling in his brain is down, and he's responding to physical stimuli but not to verbal ones.'

Kate walked home, worrying about this, knowing Angus must be frantic with concern. She found McTavish sitting forlornly on the yellow sofa and it gave her an idea.

A radical idea!

Could she do it?

Should she do it?

Perhaps it would be okay; after all, Hamish wasn't in the main ICU but in a room of his own outside the really sterile area.

She thought of the consequences, the insanitary aspects of it, then thought of a little boy that talk alone had failed to rouse from his semiconscious state.

Damn it all, it was worth a go!

'How do you feel about backpacks?' she asked the dog, remembering a friend who took her King Charles spaniel to the beach in a backpack.

She hurried inside, McTavish at her heels, and dug out a backpack that had seen better days but was still serviceable enough.

'I'll give you a run outside to do whatever you have to do,' she told him, leading him through to the backyard and chasing him around until he sniffed a bush or two and left his mark on one of them.

'Now,' she said, 'here we go.'

She lifted his chunky body, pleased he was still little more than a pup and hadn't filled out to true Highland terrier proportions.

Apparently used to being carted around by Hamish in unusual conveyances, the dog showed no objection to being treated this way.

'Okay, we're off,' she said to him, lifting him and slinging the backpack on her shoulders. With the friendly nurse on duty at the monitors she should be able to get the backpack in without question. It was Angus she was more worried about.

Would he object?

Of course he would; he'd think she was mad.

But Hamish was his child, so obviously she'd have to discuss it with him first.

She stopped next door, knocked, then explained to Juanita what she was doing.

'Angus'll have his mobile in his pocket on vibrate,' she said. 'Could you give me twenty minutes to get up there and on to the right floor, then phone him. He can't use his mobile in there, so he'll have to leave the room to check the call and I'll grab him in the foyer and explain what I want to do.'

Juanita stared at her as if she was mad, then she smiled, a broad warm smile.

'It might work,' she said. 'I can tell him I've been speaking to his mother, which is true.'

They checked their watches and Kate took off, hurrying now, as the weight of the dog on her back seemed to be increasing all the time.

From an alcove outside the PICU she saw Angus leave the unit, hurrying to the elevator foyer to answer his phone. Kate caught him as he closed the phone, drawing him into the alcove so she could explain her idea.

'That is crazy. You can't take a dog into his room—he's in a hospital bed.'

Kate looked into his eyes, aware of the plea he must be able to read in hers.

'He's not responding to anything else, Angus,' she reminded him. 'Isn't it worth a try?'

Angus's fingers had found a way into the top of the backpack and he was scratching at McTavish and murmuring to him.

'He does love the dog,' he said, his voice so rough Kate realised he was feeling pain. Pain that maybe Hamish loved his dog more than he loved his father?

'Of course he does, but a lot of that is because McTavish relies on him. Maybe thinking McTavish needs him will be the incentive to push him to the surface, back to consciousness.'

The anguish on Angus's face was so obvious Kate touched his arm, then reached up and kissed his cheek.

'Worth a try?' she said as lightly as she could, for her heart was aching for this tormented man.

'Worth a try,' he finally admitted, then he found

a smile that eased, just a little, her heartache. 'But you're the one who takes the rap if the hospital gets wind of it!' he warned, but he took the backpack off her and carried it into the room.

Once there, he grabbed a towel and put it on the side of Hamish's bed, then set the backpack on the towel. Kate held her breath as Angus opened it enough for McTavish to poke his nose and paws outside. The little dog whimpered at the sight of his master and Kate lifted Hamish's hand to rest on McTavish's head.

'It's McTavish, Hamish darling. He's come to visit you. He's been missing you so much. Won't you say hello to him?'

Kate didn't know if it was her words or the dog's rough tongue licking Hamish's hand, but the blue eyes opened and the little hand grasped one of his dog's paws as he whispered, 'McTavish.'

To Kate it was the most beautiful word she'd ever heard and she knew tears were rolling down her cheeks, down Angus's, too, she realised as he bent to take his son in his arms.

Kate tucked McTavish back into her backpack,

promised Hamish she'd visit soon, and left the room, dodging the nurse who'd entered in response to the change in Hamish's condition shown on the monitor screen.

Hamish's eyes had closed again, but through the window Kate could see that his fingers, rather than lying listlessly on the bed, were now curled around his father's hand, while Angus's free hand stroked his son's face and hair, his fingers trembling slightly.

As she left the hospital, she let McTavish out of the backpack, once again using the old belt as a lead. They walked home together, Kate pouring out her troubles to him.

'So you see, McTavish,' she finished, dropping down onto the yellow sofa and helping him jump up on it to sit beside her, 'just when the man was ready to accept that being human, which means vulnerable, was okay, this happens, and I know for sure he'll be shutting himself off from the world again—or from the world of human emotions.'

McTavish responded by putting his front paws on her lap and giving her chin a consolatory lick.

'*And* I'm going to be in trouble for taking a dog into a hospital—the one place in the world that's supposed to be a germ-free environment and who knows what germs you might have.'

McTavish was obviously bored with the conversation, as he'd now put his head on his paws, still in Kate's lap, and had closed his eyes, confirming his lack of interest with little snuffling snores. Juanita came along the footpath.

'Angus has called me. It worked, your idea?'

She was smiling with delight but Kate couldn't summon up more than a tepid grin.

'Yes, it worked,' she said, 'but I'm not sure Angus was too impressed—reckons if anyone gets into trouble it will have to be me.'

'Angus, phooey!' Juanita declared. 'He needs to be jolted out of himself that man, and though I wouldn't for the world have had this happen to Hamish, maybe it will be for the best in the long run.'

Not for me, Kate knew but didn't say.

'I hope so,' she said.

'I'm going to the hospital now,' Juanita said.

'Maybe I can nag him to come home for proper sleep.'

Then she shrugged her shoulders.

'And maybe not, but I try. You'll mind McTavish?'

Kate nodded, and watched Juanita bustle away.

'She's wrong, McTavish,' Kate told the still-sleeping dog. 'I think I managed to jolt him out of himself, just a little. But this, it's just jolted him right back to where he was.'

Alex flew home from Melbourne so Angus could take time off without leaving the teams two surgeons short, and McTavish returned to his home when Hamish came out of hospital, under strict bed-rest instructions.

Which left Kate all alone again. She went to work, and came home, phoning every evening to ask after Hamish, more often getting Juanita for the latest report but occasionally a totally formal Angus would tell her the little boy was progressing well. She longed to call in to see her young friend, but no invitation was forthcoming, so she stayed away, throwing a ball for McTavish in the evenings when he came to visit, talking to him—almost sorry the possums had left so she'd have had more company....

Baby Bob was out of the PICU and due to be medivaced back to a unit at the Port Macquarie hospital, so instead of going straight home on the Thursday afternoon, Kate made her way to the nursery to say goodbye to the Stamfords.

Bob was out of his crib, lying in his father's arms, and Kate felt such a surge of longing her knees felt weak.

'May I hold him?' she asked, and Pete Stamford handed him over. She tucked the little fellow up against her, talking quietly to him, amazed that the dark blue eyes seemed to be taking in every word she said.

'He'll be clever,' she told his beaming parents.

'Healthy is what we're after,' Mrs Stamford said. 'I was just telling Dr McDowell that a few minutes ago.'

'Dr McDowell? Here?' Kate asked, finding she

now had a churning stomach, as well as weak knees.

'Apparently his little boy's been ill and he brought up some chocolates for the staff where he'd been treated, then he heard we were going home so called in to say goodbye.'

And I missed him! Kate wailed, but she kept the words inside, then told herself it was for the best. What did they have to say to each other?

'He might be back,' Pete Stamford added. 'He said something about a present for Bob because he was the doctor's first Australian patient.'

Which means I should give this baby back to his parents and get out of here, Kate's inner messenger declared, but it was already too late, for Angus was there, a small toy wombat in his hands.

'I thought I'd seen these in the shop downstairs,' he said, speaking to the Stamfords, though his eyes had glanced towards Kate as he drew near. 'My son just adores them.'

He handed the little toy to Mrs Stamford as Kate settled the baby in his crib. He'd be travelling north by ambulance, his mother riding with him,

Pete Stamford, no doubt, driving right behind the medical vehicle.

'I'd better go. Good luck,' she said, then was surprised when Mrs Stamford reached out and pulled her into a hug.

'Thank you for everything,' the woman whispered, and Kate felt the tears that had started welling when she held baby Bob, now threatening to spill down her cheeks.

'It was nothing,' she managed to mutter, then added a general goodbye to everyone within hearing and fled the room.

Angus caught up with her in the elevator foyer where she'd been surreptitiously wiping tears from her cheeks. He came and stood beside her, not touching, or speaking, just being there. They entered the elevator together and rode it down, still silent, then, because she knew she couldn't stand the tension in this silence any longer, she broke it, asking, as they exited on the ground floor, 'How is Hamish?'

'He's fine, well enough now to be a handful as far as keeping him quiet is concerned. We've read every book ever written about possums and wombats and have moved on to platypuses and kangaroos.'

They'd moved towards the front entrance as she'd asked the question and he'd answered, but now Kate stopped, unwilling to walk home with him while her body ached to hold him, her hands to touch him, yet his whole demeanour yelled, Keep off.

'I'll drop some of my books in for him,' Kate said.

He'd stopped beside her, looking down at her, but it wasn't books he mentioned when he spoke again.

'You told me you weren't quite alone when your mother died,' he said, the words so startlingly out of context Kate frowned as she made sense of them. But making sense and saying something were two entirely different things. She could only stare at him.

'And you held that baby like he was something precious. Did you lose a child, as well? Is that what makes you long for one? Was the grandmother story just a cover?'

How had he done this?

How had Angus, of all people, swooped from swimming eyes while she held a baby, to her grandmother story being a cover in such a short time?

Confused didn't begin to cover how Kate felt, and that stirred anger.

'The grandmother story is true,' she said, and turned away, but he caught her shoulder and steered her into the café.

'Come, sit awhile with me. Talk to me, Kate. Help me here.'

She looked at him, still angry, but read a confusion to equal her own in his eyes.

Allowing him to steer her to a corner table, Kate slumped down in a chair, waited while he went to order coffee, then looked at him across the table.

'I don't think my life is any concern of yours, not any longer,' she said.

He spread his hands and shook his head.

'How else could I feel but guilty—not being home that night when Hamish first was sick? I'm not blaming you, Kate, but it brought home to me how dependent Hamish is on me, and how—'

'How you can't afford to have a life of your own because of that?' Kate demanded. Then before he could reply, she continued, the weird anger that had come from nowhere suddenly exploding. 'That's nonsense, Angus, and someone as intelligent as you should know it. It's just another excuse to hide yourself away from hurt, and don't tell me I don't know about hurt. I've felt it all, including, yes, a baby that I lost. When my mother died I was seeing a fellow student, Brian, and seeking comfort in his arms I became pregnant. He was horrified, wanted me to have a termination, but it was my baby and no way was I going to give it up, so we parted. Then two months later I miscarried. So, yes, there's more to my wanting children than my grandmother dream, but—'

'You *did* lose a child? It was a stab in the dark, when I said that, not something meant to upset you,' he said, but the stab had found its mark and suddenly Kate was too upset to stay in the café, no matter how good the coffee was. As the waitress approached with the order, Kate stood and hurried out, muttering something that might have been goodbye but was more a garbled curse.

The tears were too close again, and she was damned if she was going to cry in front of half the hospital staff....

CHAPTER TEN

'TWO COFFEES?' the waitress said, and Angus waved to her to put them down. He probably wouldn't drink either of them, but he needed to sit awhile and try to sort out some of the emotional mess curdling inside him.

Of course Kate, who'd suffered so much loss in her life, would want children of her own—a family. Not only that, she deserved a family, deserved all the happiness in the world, in fact.

The thing about Kate, he'd discovered, was that she refused to be beaten by what life threw at her. She kept going, kept smiling, always positive, always up-beat, seeing the best in situations, the best in people. She'd even tried to dig out something worthwhile in him and, to a certain extent, succeeded because he was recovering his humanity, and for that he was really grateful.

He drained his cup of coffee and started on hers, not sure where all this rational thinking was getting him, although he now had a much fuller picture of the woman he loved.

Loved?

He set the cup back carefully in its saucer, certain it had been about to slip from his grasp.

Loved?

How could he love her? He barely knew her. But even as this excuse sprang from his brain, another part of his mind was denying it. Of course he knew her, knew her from that first day at work when she'd broken through Mrs Stamford's denial, and started his own process of rehumanisation, if such a word existed.

He pictured her on the yellow sofa, an arm around his son, and remembered the stab of jealousy he'd felt, but what he should have felt was pleasure, that finally he'd found a woman who would make the ideal mother for his son.

His son!

His only child!

Kate wanted babies, wanted a family, and

knowing Kate as he now did he knew darned well one child didn't constitute a family in her terms.

And she deserved babies and a family, but was he the man to provide this? Fear grasped his heart as he considered losing Kate as he'd lost Jenna.

No, that couldn't happen!

It probably wouldn't, the scientist reminded him, but there was always that chance.

He left the coffee shop, half a cup undrunk. Alex had given him more time off, but he had patients he wanted to see—outpatients whose parents had often travelled hundreds of miles so their children could keep appointments. He wasn't going to push them on to one of the other specialists. Tomorrow he'd go to work, but taking appointments, not operating, so he'd be able to avoid Kate while he sorted things out in his head.

Avoidance was not so easy when he returned home to find her as he'd pictured her in his mind, sitting on the yellow sofa, Hamish by her side, McTavish as close as he could get to Hamish, Kate reading from a rather tattered storybook.

'This was my favourite as a child,' she said, holding it up so he could see the cover. It was a Dr Seuss book, and although he was reasonably sure Hamish had a newer and cleaner version, he could hardly complain. His son was sitting quietly, which was the main thing, and if the picture conjured up images of family in Angus's eyes, then that was his problem.

As was the distance in Kate's voice as she spoke, though when she returned to the story, she was animated once again, giving all the characters a different intonation.

The urge to join them on the yellow sofa was almost irresistible but he knew, until he'd sorted out how he felt about Kate—how could it possibly be love? He'd known Jenna for years before he'd fallen in love with her!—he had to steer clear.

On top of that was the fact that he had no idea how Kate felt about him. He had no doubt about the attraction, but love was a whole different matter. He tried to remember if she'd used words of love at any time, but knew it was a pointless exercise. If Kate had at any time mentioned love, he'd have backed off so quickly even kisses would have been off limits.

Waving a rather ineffectual goodbye, he made his way inside, but though he settled in the corner of his bedroom he'd made his study, determined to do some work, images of Kate blocked his mind. So he gave up, got the car, told Juanita he was going out for a while and headed for the beach.

He walked the coastal path, north towards another beach called Bondi, striding along until he came to a massive cemetery, perched on the edge of the cliff, gravestones looking out to sea. It was a place of such quiet beauty he found a bench and sat there, thinking of the past, reliving Jenna's death, then moving on to consider—really seriously—the future.

Needing to do something to stop herself thinking about Angus, Kate had spread drop sheets on the living-room floor, and was, rather inexpertly, rolling paint onto the uneven surface of the walls. It was a paint called white-on-white, which the man at the hardware shop had assured was perfect anywhere. What it seemed to be doing was highlight all the unevenness of the walls, and she was wondering if it was time to call in an expert when the front doorbell rang.

She looked down at the paint spatters on the old dungarees she was wearing, and frowned at the smattering of paint dots on her arms and legs, then as the doorbell pealed again, she sighed and headed for it, praying it wasn't someone important from the hospital.

'Angus?' The first word was generated by surprise, then fear took over. 'It's not Hamish, is it? He hasn't had a relapse?'

Angus shook his head, presumably answering her questions, not denying who he was.

She stared at him. He'd come to her so he must want something, but did she want him in her house?

Did she want him within a hundred yards of her, looking as she did?

Of course not, but he was there.

'Do you want to come in? It's just that I'm painting, as you can see, so it's not the best time, though what it's not the best time for, I don't know.'

The rapid heartbeats Angus's presence always caused had obviously turned her brain to mush that she was prattling on like this. And now he was smiling—more mush, although in her stomach this time.

'Not the best time for proposing, I guess,' he said softly, but she heard the words, just couldn't grasp the meaning.

'Proposing what?' she demanded, thoroughly disconcerted now.

'Marriage, of course.'

He was sounding a little tetchy now but how did 'marriage' and 'of course' get to go together?

'Marriage?' she echoed, just to make sure she'd got it right.

'Yes, marriage,' he grumbled—hardly lover-like.

'To me?'

'Of course to you.' He was snapping now.

'But I want children,' she reminded him, then suddenly realised they were still standing on her front doorstep, she completely paint-spattered, and he in shorts and a T-shirt that looked slightly damp.

'Has it been raining?' she asked, though she was sure she'd have known if it had been, but weather talk was good to get through awkward conversations.

He stepped towards her, smiling now, and put his arms around her.

'Kate, I'm proposing to you, not discussing the weather, but no, it's not raining. I just went for a walk, then needed a swim to clear my head, and it was hot so I went in fully clad—except for my shoes, of course. Now could you please put me out of my misery and tell me if you're at least interested enough in me to consider a proposal.'

He kissed her, which was a big mistake as Angus's kisses always had the effect of starting such powerful surges of desire that her mind, even when it wasn't mush, found it hard to work.

'Could you at least say something?' he asked, raising his head several minutes later. 'I'm dying here!'

'You don't want more children,' she reminded him, and he kissed her again.

'It was nothing to do with not wanting more children,' he reminded her at the next kiss break. 'It was fear for the mother of the children, and that's still there and very real and if you marry me and we have more children I shall probably drive you insane checking you for DVT after each and every birth.'

Even with a mushy brain this was beginning to sound quite hopeful, but it had all been very matter-of-fact. Was it just the attraction?

Which, given the way she was kissing him back, she'd find very hard to deny!

'Is there more?' she asked when she'd pulled away and replenished enough breath to form words.

'Of course there's more,' he told her, but he must have thought she meant more kissing because that's what happened. Eventually he broke away, this time holding her at arm's length and look-ing down at her with such tenderness she thought her heart might split in two and all her blood seep out.

'When you walked out of the coffee shop, I realised how much I loved you,' he said, his voice so deep and husky it ran across Kate's skin like the brush of butterfly wings. 'Then I thought of all I knew about you, and how you, of all people, deserve the family you crave. I knew then that even with my fear of losing another person I loved, if I married you I'd have to give you the children you deserved, because otherwise I'd lose you anyway. Does that make sense?'

Kate melted into his arms.

'Not a lot,' she whispered against his damp shirt, hoping these weren't his best casual clothes because by now they probably had quite a lot of paint on them. 'But it sounded really beautiful.'

'So, will you marry me?'

Would she?

Why the uncertainty?

Because it was so sudden?

'Oh, Angus!' She held him tight and hoped her words didn't come out as a wail. 'Do you really want this? Are you sure it's not just a reaction to Hamish's illness?'

He pushed her away again, looking deep into her eyes, studying her as if to read what she was thinking; but if *she* couldn't figure out what was going on in her head, how could he?

'I really want it,' Angus said, wondering how a decision he'd made in the cliff-top cemetery had somehow become so difficult. 'I know it won't be easy for you, taking on someone else's child, but you and Hamish seem to get on well.'

At least the smile *that* brought to her face chased away the look of worry it had held earlier, but doubts were now springing in *his* mind, bursting out like sprouting plants. She didn't love him. Couldn't think of a way to tell him, to let him down lightly! She could think of nothing worse than being Hamish's mother— Oh, hell! Perhaps he should kiss her again.

But as he tried to draw her close she held him back.

'Tell me again why you want this,' she asked.

'Because I love you,' he said, slightly puzzled as he was sure he'd told her that before.

'Really love me?' she asked, and now he *had* to kiss her. But this time he punctuated the kisses with words, telling her things he couldn't ever remembering saying before, about how wonderful she was—her empathy with patients' parents, her calm control in all situations in the operating theatre, the instinctive way she'd known that McTavish could rouse Hamish. Then the way she made him feel, ten foot tall and invincible, the way just looking at her roused his blood to fever pitch, the way thinking of her made his body hard at inappropriate times—a catalogue of love-reasons tumbling from his lips, lips that still stayed close to hers, kissing in between...

'Now it's your turn,' he finished, breathless from words *and* kisses.

She looked at him, pale green eyes alight with mischief.

'My turn to kiss you?' she teased.

'Your turn to tell me things, little witch!' he growled, his arms still loosely imprisoning her.

There was silence for what seemed forever to his overburdened heart, then she smiled a funny kind of smile that made her teeth gleam and her eyes light up.

'I love you, Angus,' she said, and that was it, but it was all he needed to hear. He drew her close again, her head resting above his heart, and held her so she could feel its excited beat, and feel the flush of heat in his body.

'That's all I need to know,' he managed, his voice so gruff with emotion he didn't recognise it as his own.

'All we need to know, as well,' another voice said, and Angus turned to see Juanita, Hamish and McTavish sitting on the yellow sofa, smug smiles on all their faces, although it wasn't really easy to read *smug* in the expression of a Highland terrier.

He frowned at all three of them but it had little effect.

'If you will propose to someone on their doorstep, you have to expect to have onlookers,' Juanita continued. 'We were actually coming over to invite Kate to Hamish's getting-better party on Saturday afternoon, and got here just in time for the show.'

Angus knew he should be angry but Kate was laughing helplessly, just standing there in paint-spattered dungarees, laughing and laughing. So instead of being angry he put his arm around her and drew her outside, stopping in front of the threesome on the sofa.

'Hamish, do you understand what's going on here?'

'You've been kissing Kate,' he said, with all the aplomb of a four-year-old who knows about kissing. 'I kissed Chloe at kindergarten—it's kind of fun.'

'I've been more than kissing Kate,' Angus said, squatting down in front of his son, praying this would go better than his proposal had—at first!

'I've been asking Kate to marry me, so that means she'll be your new mother.'

Hamish nodded, apparently shrugging off this momentous news.

'Juanita told me that ages ago,' he announced,

causing his carer to shift uncomfortably on the sofa. 'She said that Kate was just what our family needed. We just had to wait for you to figure it out for yourself. I did say I'd ask Kate for you, but Juanita said you had to ask or it wouldn't be right.'

Angus gave up squatting and collapsed onto the ground. Kate was laughing again and hugging Hamish, while Angus considered ways a doctor could get away with murder. But Juanita must have read his mind, for she reached out and touched his shoulder.

'It was in your eyes from the first time you saw her,' she said gently. 'Love like that doesn't happen often, so you have to seize it while you can. I just hoped you'd have the courage to do that, and you did. Congratulations!'

She leaned forward and kissed him on the cheek, then hugged Kate.

'Come on, Hamish, let's go back inside. We've a party to plan, then a wedding to arrange—we're going to be really busy for a while.'

They disappeared back into their house, Hamish

asking if you could have balloons at weddings and would there be cake. Kate collapsed onto the yellow sofa and smiled at the man who was pulling himself off the ground. He sat beside her and took her hand.

'It's real, then?' he asked in a bemused voice.

'I think so,' she replied, just as bemused. 'Actually, now Juanita and Hamish are in on the act, not to mention planning our wedding, I don't think we can get out of it.'

She clasped his fingers tightly as she spoke, the happiness welling so deeply inside her she needed him to anchor her to earth.

'Not to mention McTavish,' Angus reminded her, then he kissed her and she knew he was all the anchor she would ever need. In spite of all the storms she had weathered in her life, she was now safely in port.…

With Angus by her side!

EPILOGUE

BABY Hannah arrived nine months after the wedding, her father in attendance at her birth, her brother, Hamish, her first visitor. Kate held the tiny mortal in her arms, her heart so full of love for all her family she was afraid she might burst.

'Can I take her to school for show-and-tell?' Hamish asked, poking a cautious finger into his sister's rosebud mouth.

'Not this week,' Kate told him, 'but soon. She and I can both go but you'll have to have a lot of practice in holding her before we take her there.'

'Are you mad?' Angus demanded when Hamish and Juanita had departed. 'He can't take a baby to school for show-and-tell—think of the germs?'

Kate grinned at him and used their linked hands to tug him closer.

'No more fears, remember,' she said, kissing him on the lips. 'We're a glass-half-full family. In fact, in my opinion, our glass is full and running over, so stop worrying about every little thing. Now take your daughter for a walk—I need a shower before she demands another feed.'

It was a test, and Kate knew it. She also knew how hard it would be for Angus to walk out of the room, so she swung her legs out of the bed and held them up for his inspection.

'No swollen calves, no aches and pains, no redness or tenderness. I am fine, Angus, and you know it, so go.'

He kissed her again, then lifted Hannah out of her arms and left the room, walking the corridor with her, talking quietly, telling her how much he loved her, how much he loved her brother, but most of all how much he loved her mother. Telling her about family, about her grandparents who were due out from Scotland any day and how, one day, she, too, would have children and her mother would have her dreams come true—she would be a grandmother....